WAGGIT'S TALE

PETER HOWE

WAGGIT'S TALE

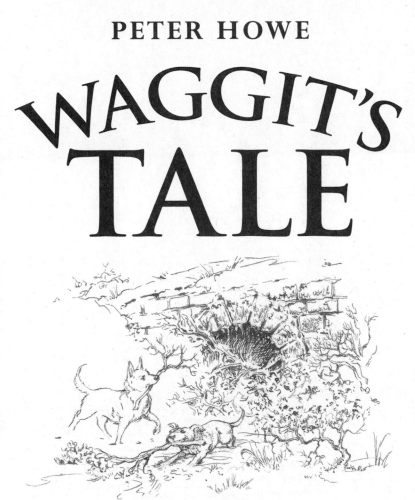

Drawings by
Omar Rayyan

HarperCollins*Publishers*

Waggit's Tale

Text copyright © 2008 by Peter Howe

Interior illustrations copyright © 2008 by Omar Rayyan

All rights reserved. Printed in the United States of America.

No part of this book may be used or reproduced in any manner
whatsoever without written permission except in the case of brief
quotations embodied in critical articles and reviews. For information
address HarperCollins Children's Books, a division of HarperCollins
Publishers, 1350 Avenue of the Americas, New York, NY 10019.

www.harpercollinschildrens.com

Library of Congress Cataloging-in-Publication Data

Howe, Peter

Waggit's tale / by Peter Howe; interior illustrations by Omar Rayyan —
1st ed.

    p. cm.

    Summary: When Waggit is abandoned by his owner as a puppy, he meets
a pack of wild dogs who become his friends and teach him to survive in the
city park, but when he has a chance to go home with a kind woman who
wants to adopt him, he takes it.

    ISBN 978-0-06-124261-8 (trade bdg.)

    ISBN 978-0-06-124262-5 (lib. bdg.)

    [1. Dogs—Fiction.] I. Rayyan, Omar, ill. II. Title.

PZ7.H8377Wag 2008   2007020878

[Fic]—dc22   CIP

                                        AC

Typography by Amy Ryan

3 4 5 6 7 8 9 10

❖

First Edition

This book is dedicated to the memory of Roo,
the real-life Waggit who was rescued from the park
to become our loyal companion for fourteen years.

ACKNOWLEDGMENTS

According to the dictionary, acknowledgments are "an author's statement of indebtedness to others." When the people who wrote the dictionary said *others* they probably meant the two-legged kind, and indeed there are many of them that I owe big-time. But leading the pack, if you'll excuse the pun, are my four-footed friends—Molly, Bill, Roo, Bobby Blue, and Rocco—each of whom, in their own ways, introduced me to the wonderful lives of dogs and showed me that living life on life's terms can be a lot of fun.

Of the many Uprights who made this book possible, gratitude should be showered on Susan Katz and Kate Jackson of Harper-Collins, who took a risk on an author unknown in the world of children's books, and also on my brilliant editor, Antonia Markiet, aka Toni, who beat my ramblings into acceptable prose. I suspect there may have been times when she wanted to beat the author as much as his prose.

Thanks should also be given to two talented dog trainers, Phyllis Couvares and Susi Nastasi, both of whom gave me a deeper understanding of canine behavior, and to Rachel McPherson of the Good Dog Foundation for providing a valuable outlet for that knowledge.

But most of all I want to thank my alpha wife, whose steady support has sustained me through all my strange endeavors, and who is probably the only person on the planet more dog-crazy than I.

Lastly thanks should always be given to those wonderful people who spend their lives rescuing dogs from the various Great Unknowns and without whom several of my dogs would not have survived long enough to give me the pleasure that they have.

PETER HOWE
Litchfield, Connecticut, 2007

TABLE OF CONTENTS

1   Lost and Found   1

2   Park Life   20

3   Cal's Calamity   39

4   The Nighthunt   58

5   Tashi's Challenge   75

6   Survival   92

7   The Cold White   104

8   Battle Plan   117

9   The Mystery of the Missing Enemy   131

10 Hidden Treasure   152

11 *Two Puppies and a Misadventure* 168

12 *Tazar's Secret* 185

13 *Captured* 198

14 *Terror in the Great Unknown* 212

15 *A New Life* 223

16 *Civilization* 236

17 *Waggit's Good-bye* 251

18 *Happy Ending* 265

Glossary 275

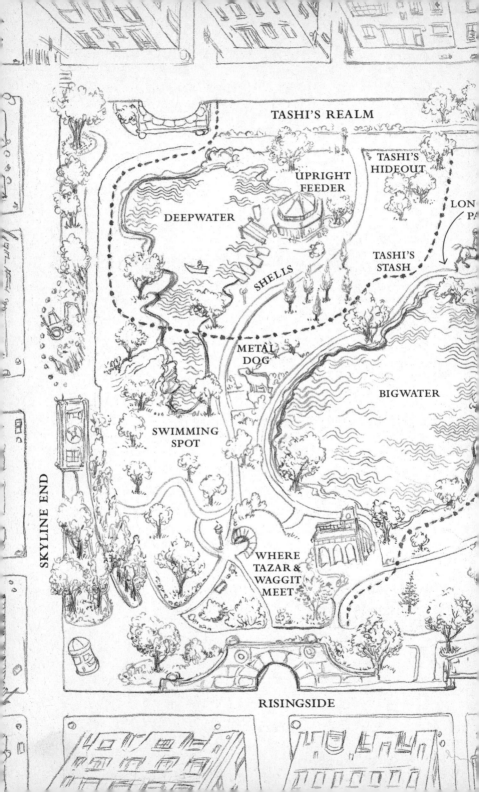

GOLDENSIDE

HALF
TOP HILL

CROSSWAY

DEEPWOODS

DEEPWOODS END

AZAR'S
REALM

WHERE
WAGGIT
MEETS
THE
WOMAN

TO THE
WOMAN'S APARTMENT

1
Lost and Found

The white puppy stopped under the bridge. He was panting hard, and his heart pounded so loudly and fast that it seemed it would burst. He could not go on anymore. He must have been running for hours, because it was quite dark now. The greenish lights of the park made cold, unfriendly shadows, like scary fingers creeping over the ground. Water dripped from a seam in the bridge and plopped into a large puddle that had collected below.

Where could his master have gone? One minute he

was there, and the next there was no sign of him. The young dog had been let off the leash—something the man had never done before, but the puppy had loved it. He'd been concentrating on a particularly interesting smell around the roots of a tree, and when he looked up, the man had disappeared. There wasn't even a trace of his scent left. The pup had looked everywhere for him, crisscrossing the open ground in his panic to find the man. The dog had raced under tunnels and over bridges, but after a while each area began to look the same, and he could not remember if he had been there before. He was lost. He was cold, lonely, and frightened.

Suddenly he heard a can being kicked, and a shadow fell across the puddle. He sprang up, his tail wagging in anticipation—his master had found him! But no, for there in front of him was a large black dog, its head tilted to one side. The puppy stood still, feeling the hair on his back and neck prickling with fear, carefully watching each movement of the dog as it walked around him, carelessly splashing through the water to complete its inspection. The young dog let out a low growl.

"Hey, friend, hackle down. I mean you no harm."

The big dog's tone was friendly, but the puppy was old enough to know that a dog's mood can change in an instant, and that under the bridge he was trapped.

"Relax, I won't hurt you. My name is Tazar, and I come out every night at this time to see if there are any brothers or sisters who are lost and need help."

"I'm not lost," the puppy said defiantly, trying to control the fear in his voice.

"You're not?"

"No. I've been running, and I'm resting here before going home."

"Oh, excuse me. I only thought—well, you sure looked lost. My mistake. I'm sorry," said Tazar.

"S'okay. I'll just be going home now."

"You know, you shouldn't be out so late; it's not safe here after dark. Tell you what, why don't I walk you to the edge of the park? I don't have anything special to do right now. Which way's your home?" Tazar asked.

The puppy nodded his head in a direction. Which direction didn't matter, since he had no idea where he was anyway. He just wanted to get to open ground, where he could run if he had to.

"Okay, friend, let's go," said Tazar.

The two dogs set off, the big one easy and strutting, his plumed black tail bobbing as he walked; the young one was nervous, wary, flinching at the noises of the small animals that skittered in the dark bushes.

"It's just a curlytail; pay it no mind."

The path wound beside a big stretch of water where a cold wind blew. They crossed a bridge, beneath which cars and buses rumbled. Finally they came to a place with a wire fence and dusty yellow patches; here the puppy had seen men and women chasing balls earlier in the day. They had walked in silence up to this point, the older dog slightly ahead, sniffing the breeze carefully. Suddenly he stopped and turned to the puppy.

"Listen, some friends of mine live near here. I'd like you to meet them."

"Thank you. That's very kind of you, and I'm sure they're very nice." The puppy did not want to offend. "But I really must get home. There are people waiting for me, and they'll be worried."

The big black dog sat down and gave him a look full of kindness and sorrow.

"My little brother," he said slowly and quietly, "I have been watching you since before the sun went down. I've seen you running across the ground as if your life depended upon it. You are lost. You know that. But now you are found, and that you don't know. You must trust me. Come, let's go and meet the friends. They're nearby."

He brushed against the white puppy so that the little fellow felt the reassuring warmth of his long black coat. He *was* lost, and he didn't know what to do next. What choice did he have other than to trust this stranger who was offering him help?

They had walked on no more than a few steps when the big dog stopped, gave two short howls, and then waited. Three howls answered them.

"Okay, let's go," said Tazar.

They ran quickly past a lamppost, off the path, down a gully, and straight into the mouth of a black tunnel. It was so dark that the puppy didn't know Tazar had stopped until he crashed into the other dog's back legs and fell over.

There was a flurry of movement and a scattering of assorted growls as he picked himself up. In the darkness he heard the big black dog say, "Brothers and sisters, we have a guest."

🍃 🍃 🍃

As the puppy's eyes got used to the darkness, he looked around and saw dogs. Lots of dogs. Dogs of all shapes and sizes. Spotty dogs and shiny dogs; thin dogs and fat dogs; timid dogs and dogs with bent ears and crooked tails who had obviously seen some rough times. They were all looking at him curiously. As he stood there, the fear returned. What if he was trapped, and these were bad dogs who would hurt him? There was no escape from the corner into which he had let himself be led. His tail wagged in terror.

Then there was a spluttering sound behind him.

"Hey, make with less of the tail, will ya!" a voice complained. He turned to see a small, wiry brown dog whose head was covered in hairs from the puppy's tail.

"Oh, excuse me," said the puppy.

The big black dog laughed a long, growling laugh. "These are my brothers and sisters, my family, my team," he said with pride.

The small brown dog came up to the puppy and sniffed his face.

"Hi. Glad to have you with us," he said. "What's your name?"

The puppy thought for a moment, puzzled.

"I don't know." He paused. "My master used to call me pooch."

"*Master!?*" the black dog roared. "*Pooch!?*"

The other dogs cowered in the face of Tazar's rage. His eyes blazed, and his lips snarled, showing huge teeth, one of which was broken halfway down, making him look even more frightening.

"These words do not exist! Not here! Not ever!"

There was total silence. Not a dog moved; each waited, fearful, scarcely breathing, for Tazar's anger to subside. Then the big black dog spoke:

"We have no masters here. We are our own masters; we owe obedience to no one. No one can take our freedom from us. As for that other word, it is so vile that no one should ever say it. It is a lie invented by Uprights so that they can feel superior to us. They know nothing of freedom. They think they are free because they cannot see the leashes that ensnare them, but the leashes are there. You and I, my brothers and sisters, proud animals of the earth, live together in true freedom and love. Our very existence pours contempt on the Uprights, on the evil Uprights."

As he finished speaking a great bellow broke from the dogs as they howled their approval. They banged their paws on the ground and their tails on the empty cardboard boxes that lay around the tunnel. Even the puppy wagged his tail ferociously and panted with enthusiasm. When the commotion died down, he looked with admiration at his new friend, Tazar.

"What *is* an Upright?" he inquired innocently.

Groans and laughter greeted this simple question, but Tazar answered him.

"Uprights, my little friend, are humans, people, owners, whatever word you have used to describe those things that strut around unnaturally on two legs. And whichever word it was, promise me you will use it no more."

"I promise," said the puppy. "I promise, I promise."

"One promise is enough." The black dog chuckled. "Keep some promises for yourself."

"So what do we call him?" the brown dog asked.

"We will give him a name," Tazar said. "It will be our present to welcome him to the team. Now what shall it be?"

A murmur passed through the group. The puppy was sniffed. One dog gnawed noisily on an old bone to speed his thoughts along, then said between chews, "He's very white."

"His ears are awful big," said one of the lady dogs.

"He sure has a powerful tail," said the scruffy brown dog.

The puppy turned his head to look at his tail. It certainly did seem too big for his body, and kind of ugly. He flattened his ears against his head in shame. Tazar looked sternly at the scruffy brown dog, whose own name was Lowdown.

"It's nobody's fault if he or she has a large tail, or even"—he looked meaningfully at Lowdown—"short legs."

"It's not the size of his tail that's the problem," the brown dog said. "It's just that when you're my height and standing behind him, it's better if he doesn't wag it."

The bone-chewing dog paused and looked up for a moment.

"Waggit? Did you say his name was Waggit?"

"No, I didn't." Lowdown thought for a moment. "But it could be, and maybe it should be. Waggit."

Tazar rolled the name around his mouth as if tasting it.

"Waggit. Mmmm, I like it. Waggit. It pleases me. It suits. Waggit it is then."

"Waggit." "Waggit." "Waggit." Each of the friends said it, trying it out. "Waggit." "Waggit." They began to dance around him, barking out his name, over and over again. One by one they came to him, licked him, nuzzled him, and some even bit him playfully. They whispered his name in his ear, and the puppy felt happier and prouder than he ever had in his life. These were his new friends. This was his new name. His tail wagged so hard it seemed ready to come off. Even when it hit Lowdown in the face again, the little dog didn't complain.

Then Tazar cleared his throat.

"Now that we know your name, you should know all of ours," he said, and stretched out his front legs as if to bow. This caused a big ruff to stand up behind his head, making him appear noble and warlike. "Come, friends, let's introduce ourselves."

Each dog went up to Waggit, and their names came tumbling out; "Raz" and "Cal" and "Lady Magica." Lowdown told Waggit that he didn't really like his name, but the others found it cute, so he put up with it. Then there was "Gruff," who seemed bad tempered and muttered something about there being yet another mouth to feed, and "Gordo" who was funny and fat.

The names flew into Waggit's head, spun around a couple of times, and flew straight out again.

Not all the dogs came up to him however. One lay at the far end of the tunnel and hadn't moved the entire time that Waggit had been there. She was long, thin, and elegant, the most beautiful dog he had ever seen. Her delicate face was fringed with tufts of soft, wispy hair. She wore a jeweled collar around her neck, from which some of the stones were missing.

Tazar pushed Waggit toward her.

"May I present," he said, very formally, "the Lady Alicia."

Lady Alicia regarded the puppy with a cold, haughty look.

"Howdja know he ain't from Tashi's team? Eh? I mean howdja know he ain't a spy?"

Waggit cocked his head to one side. He could not understand how that screeching voice could come from such a beautiful dog.

"Do you really think that Tashi is clever enough to send a frightened little creature like this to spy on us? That would require a level of intelligence that he just doesn't have. Don't you think we could tell one of Tashi's spies before he got to the Bigwater? He's just not that clever and never will be."

The Lady Alicia sulked. "Well, I don't think you should pull in every dumb dog what gets lost and bring 'em back here. It's too crowded already. There just ain't no privacy."

"We can't leave him out there," Tazar replied. "He's your brother as well as mine."

"From the look of him he's just about everybody's brother *except* mine," she said scornfully.

Lady Alicia had obviously gone too far, for Tazar fixed her with his blazing eyes.

"Well, we don't all have the benefit of a pedigree so kindly given to us by Uprights!" he said, and then walked away from her. Waggit followed him, nervously looking over his shoulder. He seemed to have made an enemy in the Lady Alicia, but he didn't know how or why.

During this exchange the other dogs had retreated to the mouth of the tunnel. Tazar strode up to them, his mood the same color as his coat.

"Get the food," he said curtly.

There was a flurry of movement as each dog dragged the items he or she had collected during the day into the middle of the floor. There was some old bread that was hard and had a green edge to it; half a bag of potato chips; most of an apple; three pieces of hot dog; a whole pretzel; two pieces of fried chicken; and a slice of pizza with little spaces where the sausage had been. A young, agile-looking dog called Raz waited until all of this had been assembled, and then, with a proud swagger, placed three large slices of good ham on top of it all.

"Had to fight a Skurdie for them," he said, as nonchalantly as he could.

The growls of admiration for this achievement stopped when Cal revealed that there had been four slices, and that the Skurdie had been so frightened by the two dogs that he had run away immediately. Raz scowled at his friend, and pointed out that when all was said and done there were still three good slices of ham, which was true.

Tazar looked at the pile of goodies in front of him. With one paw he pulled out the whole pretzel and examined it carefully.

"Whose is this?" he asked.

"Mine, boss. I got it," said Gordo.

"How?"

"It fell off the back of a cart."

Tazar said nothing but raised one eyebrow and one ear.

"Honest, I swear to you," Gordo whined, "the Upright was getting out a whole bunch to put over the heat and he dropped this one. I mean, it almost rolled into my mouth."

"You'd better be right, Gordo. There's nothing that gets the Ruzelas out quicker than dogs attacking food vendors."

"Me, attack! I don't attack. I'm a retriever, not an attacker," Gordo said, outraged.

"That's true enough," said Gruff. "He won't even attack his own fleas."

The mere mention of the word caused Lowdown to go into a spasm of scratching. Tazar laughed and then nodded to Gordo.

"Okay, divide it up."

Gordo very carefully and delicately separated the food into little piles, neatly biting the bigger pieces of ham and pizza into smaller segments.

Waggit sidled up to Cal. "What is a Skurdie?" he asked.

"Skurdies? They're sort of halfway between Uprights and us. I mean they are upright, all right, but they don't live in buildings. They live in the park and sleep under bushes. They get their food out of garbage cans just like we do. I think they'd like to be the same as us, but they just don't know how."

"Is Tashi a Skurdie?" asked Waggit.

All the dogs who heard this question howled with laughter and nudged the ones who hadn't. "Tashi, a Skurdie!" they said, causing more laughter.

"The way Tazar tells it, Tashi ain't good enough to be a Skurdie," said Cal, panting with amusement. "He's actually a dog who's the boss of another team that lives on the Goldenside of the park, and he's bad. We won't have nothing to do with him. He wants our realm to add to his, so when he comes over here we have to tussle."

This sounded frightening and dangerous to Waggit, so he didn't ask what tussling involved. Besides that, Gordo had finished dividing the food into a circle of nine piles.

"Brothers and sisters, on your places," Tazar commanded.

The dogs scuttled around, bumping into one another in their eagerness to get to their meal. Waggit watched, not quite sure what to do. Every dog had a spot in the circle. When they got there they sat and turned toward Tazar. Just to the left of the leader was one pile without any dog beside it.

"Come, little brother," Tazar said. "This is your place, and this is your food. Come sit."

"But I didn't find any food like the others did," Waggit protested, although he could feel the hunger rumbling around his stomach. "Why should you give me any of yours?"

"That's the way we do things around here. Each one helps the other. Maybe tomorrow Raz won't find a thing, and you'll go out hunting and come back with a fat scurry, or maybe a curlytail. I've got a feeling that you're going to be a fine hunter!"

Gruff was hungry and getting impatient with all this chatter. "Go sit down. I want to eat."

So the puppy went to his place and sat. The food looked so delicious he could hardly wait. He was about to wolf it all down when he felt Tazar's paw on his. The black dog lifted his head and in a soft howl said:

"Remember as you eat, you eat your brother's food; remember as you sleep, you take your sister's space; remember as you live, your life belongs to them. You are the team; the team is you. The two are one; the one is two."

As the last words were spoken, the hungry dogs attacked the little mounds. The only sounds were the chomping of jaws and the smacking of lips. The Lady Magica bit into a piece of hot dog.

"Ugh. Sauerkraut. It's always covered in sauerkraut. Doesn't anyone have onions and mustard anymore?" she asked.

"No," said Lowdown, "they were all sauerkraut. It's probably why they were thrown away in the first place."

"I hope," Gruff said gloomily, "that Tazar's right about Waggit's hunting potential. We haven't had fresh meat in an age."

The Lady Alicia delicately ran an elegant tongue around her elegant nose.

"I wouldn't betcha collar on it," she squawked. "That dog's so scared the curlytails'll probably end up eating him."

"Curlytails don't eat meat. They only eat tree nuts and bread. It's a well-known fact," Gruff replied.

Gruff's remark came as a relief to the puppy, who had been listening to the group's expectations of him with alarm. He had no idea what a curlytail was, but he was glad they were vegetarians. He had never hunted. In fact the only thing he'd ever chased had been the ball his master, the Upright, had thrown for him. But the food had given him a warm and sleepy feeling. He didn't want to think about tomorrow until tomorrow. He lay down, gave a soft belch, and looked around. Along the sides of the tunnel there was an assortment of boxes, mostly filled with newspapers and bits of rags. The back entrance was covered over in trees and bushes that protected the dogs from weather and intruders.

At the front end there was a lamppost, whose light would reveal any interloper before he could get too close. Whoever had chosen this as the team's home had known exactly what to look for and had found it. This gave the puppy a good, safe feeling. Not that he intended to spend the rest of his life here. Everyone was very nice, except for the Lady Alicia and Gruff, but in his heart he felt he belonged to his master. *Yes, he thought, he is my master. I'm sure he'll come back to the park tomorrow, and find me and take me back to the mistress and their baby, and I won't ever have to worry if I can hunt or not.* This thought was so comforting that he stretched, yawned, and let his eyes slowly close.

Tazar came over to the sleeping puppy.

"Who's doing eyes and ears tonight?" he asked the group.

"Me, boss," said Lowdown. "It's my turn."

"No, you stay with the kid," Tazar said, nodding toward Waggit. "I'll take the watch. He'll need some warmth before the morning. Don't wake him up to move him to your box; just pull some paper over you both. And Lowdown . . ."

"Yes, boss?"

"Just remember how you felt the day that you were abandoned."

"Yes, boss, I ain't never going to forget it," the little dog said sadly, and settled down beside the young, thin body already twitching with terrible dreams.

2
Park Life

Waggit awoke with a start. At first he couldn't remember where he was, and for a while he couldn't decide whether he was dreaming. He looked around to see that most of the other dogs were still sleeping, half in and half out of their boxes, some stretched out regally, others wound up into tight little balls. Cal and Raz shared the same box. Gordo's was too small for him, and his head took up a lot of space in Lady Magica's. Closest of all was Lowdown, whose wiry little body was pressed next to Waggit's own. Without waking, Lowdown yawned, and the puppy could see two large blue spots, like ink blots, on the other dog's tongue. Very carefully Waggit got up and stretched. Outside the mouth of the tunnel, the park was shrouded in a white mist. It looked strange and unreal, not at all the sort of place you'd want to call home.

Gathering his courage, he walked out. The sun was up now, pale and thin, filtering a soft amber light through the mist, but as yet giving no warmth. The light sparkled off the frost on the leaves that crunched beneath his paws as he climbed up the bank to the path. When he got there he stopped and let his senses feel the air. His ears listened to the waking city, the low rumble of the traffic and the bad-tempered sounds of car horns. His nose picked up the sharp smells of the coming winter, the cold wet breeze from a lake, and from somewhere else a drift of smoke. Then came the animal smell of a human, strong and getting stronger. Waggit could hear the sound of footsteps on the path. He scuttled behind a bush as a precaution and waited with both fear and excitement. His master didn't usually get up this early, but he may not have been able to sleep if he was worried. Waggit imagined him tossing and turning in his bed until he got dressed and came out to find his lost dog.

The human gradually appeared through the mist—a man with a hat pulled down over his head, collar up, and shoulders hunched against the cold. It wasn't his master; it was just someone who wanted to get from one place to another, disappearing into the mist as quickly as he had appeared. Waggit sighed and returned to the path.

"You did well, little brother." It was Tazar's voice, but the puppy couldn't see him. He cocked his head to get a better fix as the voice continued.

"If you care to live, you must live with care. We have many enemies." Waggit still could not see where the dog was hidden.

"Come up here above the tunnel," Tazar said.

Waggit looked around. To his right there was a path, which led to a sort of bridge that formed the top of the tunnel and was covered with bushes and scrubby trees that were thick and nearly impenetrable, even without their leaves. Waggit took this path and started to climb. A wire trash basket lay on its side, and the mass of soda cans and paper that had spilled out of it blocked the narrow track. Waggit leapt across these, then hopped awkwardly over tree roots and crawled flat on his stomach under the low bushes until he came to the top.

"Through here, my friend," came Tazar's voice.

He could just see Tazar's head in a patch of thick brush, and he plunged toward it. It was surprisingly easy to get through, and he found to his amazement that he and the black dog were in a kind of cave formed from brushes and branches. There was a clear view of the path in both directions, or there would have been if the mist had lifted.

"I couldn't see you from down there," Waggit said.

"That," said Tazar proudly, "is the whole point. There's no use keeping watch if your enemies see you before you see them."

"Who're you looking for?" the puppy asked.

"As I said, we have many enemies," the leader replied.

Waggit was hoping that Tazar would be a bit more precise on the subject of enemies so that he would know what to look out for.

"But who are they, and what will they do to us?" he insisted.

"Mmmm. First there's Tashi's team. Now, they're not as bad as they think they are, but they want our realm, because they live on the Goldenside, where there're too many Uprights, too many rollers, the air stinks, and there's just not the space we've got here. They think if they come over here we'll go whimpering off and leave it all to them. But we've beaten them often, so they don't come around as much anymore. Tashi knows that a boss can only be beaten so many times and still be a boss."

So far the enemies didn't sound all that bad.

"Who else?" Waggit asked.

"Well, there are the Stoners. They're Uprights, only they're not full Uprights, and they're not puppy Uprights either, but sort of in between. Stoners are bad and they're mean. They come in packs and throw rocks at you or hit you with sticks or cover you in bad water and set fire to you. If they catch you they'll cut you with silver claws. They got one sister, and they cut her so badly she just died in her box." The memory made Tazar sad.

Waggit trembled. The Stoners sounded terrible, and they might not even be the worst. He took a deep breath and stammered, "Are there any m-m-more?"

"Oh, yes. There is no shortage of enemies. Watch out for the Ruzelas. You can always tell them because they wear different coats from the other Uprights, so they all look the same. Sometimes they wear funny hats, too. We'll see if we can find some today so you'll know what they look like."

"What do Ruzelas do?" asked Waggit.

"They don't like us living in the park. Why, I don't know; but a dog without an Upright seems odd to them. They think we should be back in slavery, snug as a bug in front of some Upright's fire."

Snug as a bug sounded pretty good to Waggit, but he didn't say it. Instead he asked, "But what do they actually do to you?"

"They try to catch you. They aren't too good at it, and mostly they don't bother unless you're sick or you snapped your leg or something like that. But if you bite an Upright, even if the Upright was attacking you and you only did it in self-defense, then they really come after you. When they catch you they give you to some other Ruzelas who come in big rollers and take you away."

"Where do they take you?" Waggit asked nervously.

"Nobody knows, because nobody's ever come back. Wherever it is, it's permanent. Now, I'm not saying I know what they do when they get you to wherever they take you, but it seems to me that there's only one thing that's really permanent; there's only one thing you never come back from."

"What's that?" asked Waggit, although he'd really rather not know.

"Death, little brother," Tazar replied quietly. "Death."

Waggit sighed and lay with his head between his paws, and thought about how dangerous life had become, and how quickly. Only a day ago it had been so comfortable, so safe.

In a mournful voice he said, "What can we do, I mean, if they come, the Ruzelas and the Stoners? What *can* we do?"

"We can run. You and I can move faster than any Upright; even Lowdown can if he gets a bit of a start. So that's what we do, we run and scatter, and then we meet, not here but at another place we've got." He looked at the young dog. "Be cheerful, little one. It works. We're not going to lose you; don't worry."

Waggit was not so sure.

"How do we know if an enemy's coming?"

"We use our senses—eyes, ears, and noses. Each night one of us stays here and waits and watches to make sure the team sleeps tight and safe."

"What if someone comes?" continued Waggit.

"So many questions from such a small brother. If somebody comes, why, then we sound the alarm." Tazar pointed with his nose to the far side of the bridge, where eight or ten soda cans had been placed on top of the balustrade. A sly grin broke out on his face as he looked at Waggit.

"You know, those dogs should be up by now. They're getting awful lazy. Why don't you and I see how sharp they can be?"

He moved quietly to where the cans were, then quickly ran his tail along them, causing them to fall with a clatter and a clang into the back entrance of the tunnel. Instantly Tazar and Waggit heard muffled sounds of panic and confusion. They watched as the dogs burst out of the tunnel and scuttled along secret paths over the hill and out of sight. The last to leave was Lowdown, his little legs flying so fast that it seemed as if he should be covering twice as much ground as he actually was. Tazar chuckled his wicked laugh.

"See, I told you, all he needs is a bit of a start."

It took Tazar and Waggit several minutes to get to the meeting place. The mist had cleared, and warmth was finally coming to the park. Waggit almost felt happy as he trotted along beside Tazar. A couple of times the puppy fell behind to try to imitate the black dog's swagger, but his paws seemed too big and his legs too long. And Waggit didn't have a magnificent plumed tail that bobbed and fluttered with each step, like the flag of a general. So he contented himself with sniffing interesting smells, attacking windblown leaves, and casting a careful eye over anybody who looked even vaguely like his master.

The rest of the dogs had assembled at a place called Half Top Hill. Tazar proudly told Waggit that this was the scene of the last and most humiliating defeat of Tashi's team, which had retreated in disarray when the Tazarians rolled three large trash barrels down the long slope at them. "Trash beating trash," was how he put it.

Even Waggit realized that this would be an easy place to defend. The only way up was the long slope that the barrels had gone down, the other sides of the hill being much too steep to climb. There were good views all around, one over the field where people chased balls, and another along the road to the Risingside. All around the hill was a crunchy black path for horses, and any dog with a pair of ears worth the name could hear somebody walking on that.

In fact the waiting dogs had seen Waggit and Tazar approaching long before they arrived. They crowded around with worried faces.

"What was it, boss?"

"Who'd you see?"

"Are you okay?"

"Did they follow you?"

"Everybody relax," said Tazar. "I think we lost them. Well, I think we lost the first two groups anyway."

"Who were they?"

"Ruzelas, but Ruzelas like you've never seen before. As tall as trees they were, with green faces, and red beams of burning light coming out of their eyes. They had long claws, and they carried sticks with silver hooks on them."

As Tazar told his tall story each dog backed away from him. Eyes wide and hackles up, they edged toward one another, packing together for protection.

"As they walked," Tazar continued, warming to his fantasy, "the ground shook and the sky grew dark. I tell you, they were awesome."

There was total silence as the dogs tried to imagine such monsters. Suddenly Lowdown cocked his head to one side and looked inquisitively at Waggit.

"'Scuse me for saying this, boss, but if they was that awesome, how come this skinny little white thing, who ain't the bravest animal I've ever met, is sitting all calm and relaxed, when by rights he should be halfway up this tree calling for his mama?"

"Maybe this skinny little white thing's braver than you think," Tazar replied.

"Well, maybe he is, and maybe he ain't, but I've got an itch"—and he scratched himself as if to prove the point—"and my itch tells me that maybe them Ruzelas wasn't quite as scary as you said. In fact maybe they wasn't Ruzelas at all. In fact maybe they wasn't anything at all."

Tazar (who had been looking quite awesome himself during the telling of the tale) sat down and grinned at the scruffy little dog.

"There are times, Lowdown, when I reckon you're the smartest one on the team."

The Lady Alicia's screech shattered the air.

"What are you two talking about? Are we going to

be murdered in our beds or ain't we? I mean, I'd like to know."

"My dear lady," Tazar said in his most reassuring tone, "while I'm here you will be murdered neither in your bed nor out of it. This morning's actions were a test, just to see if the system was working; and I tell you, it worked perfectly. The story I added to make life more interesting."

"A test!" Gruff grumbled. "You got me out of my bed, with the aches I've got in my bones; you make me climb this mountain, with a chest like I've got; you expose me to the cold and then scare me half to death with some cockamamie tale. You do all this for a test!"

"We saw you scampering up that hill, didn't we, little brother?" Tazar asked Waggit. "And you were up there with the best of them. Those aching old bones did you a service when you thought your life depended upon it."

"Well, I'm with Gruff," said Alicia. "You've got no right to go around scaring folks like that. As it was I had a terrible night, and I'd only just got off to sleep. I'm going to go back now and see if I can snatch a few more minutes of rest before something else disturbs me."

Since Alicia was famous for being able to sleep anywhere and at any time, this last statement produced
muffled snorts and woofs from the rest of the team,
which she haughtily ignored. With her beautiful head
held high she delicately picked her way down the hill
on her long, elegant legs.

"You mean there never was any danger, Tazar?"
Lady Magica asked.

"The only danger was that you would sleep too
long and miss the beauty of this day," said Tazar.

"Oh, Tazar, you are naughty. We were all so scared.
But it was a good story!" Magica giggled.

Tazar shrugged his shoulders and huffed a bit in an
attempt to be modest, which was never easy for him.

"I'd have protected you, Magica; if there'd been any
danger, that is," said Gordo, who was irritated by her
adoring looks at Tazar. Lady Magica raced up to him
playfully.

"No you wouldn't!" She laughed. "'Cause you're a
great big lazy lump." She nipped him affectionately on
the ear.

"Ow, that hurt," he said. "It really did." And then he
sighed because he had loved Magica for a long time.

"Some protector," she said. "Come on. If you want

to protect me you have to catch me first." And with that she leapt agilely down the steep side of the hill, hopping from tree root to rock, until she disappeared into the woods.

Gordo lumbered after her, tumbling and crashing down the last part of the incline, and landing with an awful bang beside the path, which he crossed, but not before nearly colliding with a man on a bike, who shouted terrible things to him as he, too, disappeared into the woods.

"I really don't know what's going to become of that boy," Gruff complained. "He doesn't seem to have a brain between his ears, and as for his manners . . ." Gruff's voice trailed off as if Gordo's manners were beyond description. "But when you get to my age," he continued, "nothing seems as good as it used to be, particularly the way young puppies behave."

This last remark was directed toward Waggit and was accompanied by a stern look.

"Well," Gruff sighed, "might as well face up to whatever discomforts the day will bring. Best to meet them head-on, I always say, except for the ones that take you by surprise early in the morning."

And on that note of disapproval he slowly walked

away with the limp that only seemed to bother him when he was feeling truly sorry for himself.

Gruff's departure left five dogs on the hill. Two of them, Cal and Raz, had spent most of their time doing what they did best: wrestling with each other, rolling over and over until they were both covered in dead leaves, bits of twig, and a lot of mud. They had called a time-out through sheer exhaustion, and now, their tongues hanging out, they stood looking toward Tazar for something else to do.

"I'm going to the Skyline End," Tazar said, nodding toward the tall buildings that fringed one end of the park. "Yesterday I saw lots of Uprights digging holes with those big scooper machines that eat the earth. Uprights that dig holes always have a lot of food. Besides, I want to see what they're doing. I mean, once they start, you never know where they'll dig holes next. You two coming?" he said to Cal and Raz. They were still panting too much to say anything but nodded their heads in agreement.

"What about us, boss? Me and Waggit?" said Lowdown, who, like many short people, was always sure that he was being left out of things.

"You take Waggit and show him the park. Show him

where to go and where not to go. Show him what a Ruzela looks like, and where Tashi's ground is, but don't go too close."

"Okay, boss." Lowdown could not hide the disappointment in his voice.

"And, Lowdown, find out if he can hunt."

"I'll do my best," he said without much enthusiasm.

"Are you all right with that, Waggit?" Tazar asked the puppy.

"Yeah, that's great, 'cause I want to see if I can find my own . . . Upright. He'll probably be looking for me."

Waggit had been about to say "owner" but had caught himself just in time. He hoped they hadn't noticed, but he suspected, from the way they ignored what he said, that they had.

"We'll be off then," said Tazar. "You two take care of yourselves, and have a nice day."

Tazar, Cal, and Raz went down the hill, running at full tilt until they disappeared from sight.

Lowdown looked at Waggit. "What do you want to do first?" he asked.

Waggit wasn't used to making decisions. Until yesterday everything had been planned for him; his life had been ordered and easy.

Sensing this, Lowdown said, "I'd better show you the lines."

He took a stick in his mouth and carefully dragged it through the mud to make a map. He outlined a long, thin rectangle, and about two thirds of the way up, he drew a large blob.

"Aserigawter," he said with the stick still in his mouth.

"Pardon?" said Waggit.

Lowdown dropped the stick and repeated, "That's the Bigwater."

"Oh," said Waggit, as the mapmaker looked down to see that the Bigwater had just become bigger, on account of the stick landing on it. It now took up nearly all the rectangle.

"Tell you what, I'll draw all the lines and then tell you what they are."

On a new rectangle he marked the big blob again, and about a third of the way up he drew a smaller one, with two even smaller ones beside it. At the top end there were three blobs all joined together, and he finished up with a tiny one in the very bottom corner. When he was done he threw away the stick with a toss of his head.

"Now pay attention," he said. "This is the Bigwater, and this here"—he pointed to the second biggest blob—"is the Deepwater, where the Uprights go floating in big wooden shells. We go floating there, too, when it's warm enough, only we don't need the shells. Now this here's the Goldenside, where Tashi lives, and this part's the Risingside, where we live, and that's the Skyline End. That's dangerous. Lots of Uprights and lots of Ruzelas. This end's the Deepwoods, and that's safer because there's more cover and hardly any Uprights."

Lowdown paused and looked at the worried frown on Waggit's face.

"Are you getting all this?" he asked.

"Yes . . . well, no," Waggit replied.

"What don't you understand?"

"You say that this is the Bigwater, but it's not. The Bigwater's over there; you can almost see it from here. This isn't water anyway; it's just a bit of mud."

"No, no, no. I'm not saying this *is* the Bigwater. I'm saying this is what the Bigwater *looks* like. If you was a flutter, and you was fluttering about in the sky, and you looked down on the park, this is what it would look like."

At this point Waggit was frowning so much in his efforts to understand that his forehead actually hurt. Lowdown stomped his paws somewhat angrily on the muddy drawing and said, "I think we're going to have to take you around and show you places, 'cause I don't know what other things you're good at, but getting lost sure is one of them."

3
Cal's Calamity

The two dogs set off on the journey of education and exploration. Waggit was happy to be out in the open parkland. The dangers of yesterday were less frightening today, and he felt sure that, whatever happened, Tazar could be relied upon to put things right. He liked Lowdown. The little dog seemed brave and smart, someone who wouldn't abandon you if things went wrong. But the thing that was uppermost in Waggit's mind was the hope of finding his master.

As they left the hill behind, Lowdown seemed much

more nervous. The smallest noise made him prick up his ears or stop suddenly. He kept to the edge of the paths, going at a steady but fast pace, not exactly running, but making sure they never stayed in one place too long. There were more Uprights around now, and every time they came near one, Lowdown would branch off into the field or woods to avoid them. When this happened he continued with the same steady trot, his head always forward, never meeting the human's eyes. Waggit looked up each time, hoping to see the friendly face of his master.

They had gone down the Risingside, past the tunnel, past the Bigwater, over a bridge where cars rumbled below, and across a small field with the horse path on one side and the road on the other, when Lowdown stopped. He listened for a few seconds, then raced up a low hill, plunged into some bushes, and lay flat. Waggit followed closely behind, crawling on his stomach until their heads met.

"What's happening?" Waggit began, but Lowdown silenced him with a soft growl. Then Waggit heard the clopping sound of two horses being ridden by park rangers along the path directly below where the dogs lay hidden. As slowly and quietly as possible, Lowdown began to edge away from their vantage point, with Waggit close on his tail, until both dogs were free of the undergrowth that had protected them and in open ground. Then they ran as fast as their legs would allow to a clearing where a large rock hung over the Deep-water. Here they stopped to catch their breath.

It was a few minutes before they were able to speak without panting. Finally Waggit said, "Who were they, those Uprights?"

"Ruzelas. Ruzelas on longlegs. Holy Bones, those longlegs are stupid. I thought petulants were pretty stupid, but at least they don't let Uprights bounce around on their backs like that."

"Did they see us, the Ruzelas?"

"No, but longlegs are dangerous. They're fast, faster than any of us. A Ruzela on a longleg is about the only thing in the park that even Alicia can't outrun."

The sun was filtering through the bare branches of the trees and gently warming the rock upon which they lay. Waggit rested his head on his front paws, sighed, and was quite happy to stay in this spot, which seemed comfortable and safe. Lowdown had other plans, but inside his head the plans and his conscience were having a battle.

He wanted to be with Tazar, Cal, and Raz, for wherever those three were there was always fun and excitement. He realized that he couldn't run as fast as they could, but he was smart and cunning, and had good ideas, all of which he thought should count for something more than puppy-sitting!

Not that he had anything against Waggit, who seemed nice but at the moment was deadweight as far as Lowdown was concerned. Apart from being very young, up until yesterday Waggit had been a pet. Lowdown could just imagine him lying on his back with his legs in the air, waiting for his stomach to be tickled. The thought sent a shudder through the older dog's body.

Lowdown wanted to go down to the Skyline End to join the other three, but Tazar had put him in charge of Waggit, who was not yet a team dog and did not have team dog instincts. To take an animal like this to the Skyline End would be dangerous. He finally decided on a compromise.

"I think we should show you some more of the park," he said to Waggit as casually as he could.

Waggit, who had nearly fallen asleep, woke up suddenly, and said, "Well, okay, if it's not too much bother."

"No, I think it will be good for you. We'll go to the Skyline End first. Now that part of the park is a bit tricky on account of the number of Uprights and Ruzelas that are always there. So what we'll do is go round the Deepwater on this side, where there's more woods, then cut across the path by the road, and then a bit farther on there's a big rock that you can get a real good view from. I can point out all the things you should know and we won't have to go into the worst bits at all."

Although this didn't sound like a particularly great plan to Waggit, it did sound a lot better than going into the worst bits, so he agreed. Lowdown himself didn't think it was one of his best ideas, but it was all he could come up with for now. At least he would be able to find out what was going on at the Skyline End, and with a bit of luck he would spot the Tazarians and see what they were doing.

And so they set off. When they got to it, the big rock was huge, and it sat in the ground at a crazy angle, like an old man's tooth. It was hard to climb because their claws kept slipping on its hard gray surface, but they finally got to the top, where they rested and admired the view of the Skyline End. From here they could see the tall buildings, the people, and the roads, where cars and yellow taxis snaked their way along. On one side was the area where the children played, swinging, screaming, and fighting, for all the world like puppies. On the other side were the workers that Tazar had mentioned, and their huge machines that smashed and scooped the earth. They were big men, many with large stomachs, and they wore hard hats on their heads, some bright red, others blue. Their machines were silent now, resting in the middle of the day, and the men were sitting around eating food that they had brought from home in brown paper bags or shiny metal lunch boxes. They were relaxed and laughing as they ate and drank.

Suddenly Waggit's ears went up. "Look," he said, "there's Tazar, Cal, and Raz."

"Where? I don't see them." Lowdown peered, straining to see with his older eyes.

"There, you see, where the longlegs are."

A line of carriage horses stood waiting for customers, stomping their feet and blowing streams of hot air through their large nostrils. Tazar, Cal, and Raz moved past them in the same way that Lowdown went through the park, at a steady pace, ears down, tails between legs, looking straight ahead and making eye contact with nobody.

"Okay, I see them. I think they're coming this way. We'll join them when they get here." Lowdown was pleased that his plan had worked out so well.

The three dogs did appear to be coming toward the big rock. They were now at the point where the path came closest to the diggers. Suddenly Cal broke away from the other two, and with an astonishing burst of speed dashed toward one of the open boxes full of food. There was a shout of anger from the Upright whose box it was, but Cal was too quick for him. He was now racing back to the other two with a huge sausage in his mouth. He would have got away with it had he not dropped his prize halfway to safety. At this point he was going at such speed that he should have left it there and rejoined his friends, but having made the swipe, and motivated by a deep hunger, he turned and went back.

Again he nearly made it, but just as he was about to pick up the sausage one of the men threw something that landed within inches of it with the crashing sound of breaking glass. A white froth foamed up from the shattered bottle and quickly turned crimson as Cal, unable to stop in time, trod on a shard of glass that cut deep into the pads of his front paw.

He let out a howl of pain, and ran back to Tazar and Raz as fast as his remaining three legs would take him, leaving a trail of blood as he went. The workman came forward, picked up the sausage with one hand, and with the other took a long stick from a pile on the ground. The other men, seeing what had been going on, also picked up sticks and rocks and advanced menacingly on the dogs.

As soon as Tazar saw the danger he leapt in front of Cal, his black hackles standing up in an angry mane, his top lip pulled back in a vicious sneer, showing long white fangs. His brown eyes blazed with hatred and contempt for these creatures on two legs that dared to injure one of his brothers. The dog's fury stopped the men in their tracks. Raz joined Tazar, and the two of them made stabbing little forays, testing the enemy's courage.

"Let's go," said Lowdown. He hurled his little body down the rock and across the open ground in a straight line toward his companions. Waggit followed and overtook the small brown dog in no time. He got to where Cal was limping across the field, and saw the pain in the injured animal's eyes. He was about to join Raz and Tazar when he caught sight of the man's face. It was so full of contempt and anger that Waggit could not move, his legs frozen by fear, his tail swishing back and forth with anxiety.

Lowdown came barreling up, panting so hard that he could barely speak.

"Go on," he urged, "help them."

Still Waggit could not move.

"Can't you see, Waggit?" said Lowdown. "They're terrified of us. Go in and help. You'll come to no harm."

Summoning all the courage he had, Waggit joined the other two, snapping and snarling, and although he was ready to retreat at full speed in an instant, he helped put up a good enough show to stop the Uprights in their tracks, giving Lowdown and Cal time to get away.

"Under the wooden bridge by the Deepwater," Lowdown yelled as they made good their escape. "Meet us there."

The three remaining dogs held their ground for several minutes longer until Tazar said, "Run." And run they did, faster than the wind, their legs stretched as far as they would go, ears and tails flying, leaving the Uprights foolishly standing with sticks in their hands and nothing to shake them at.

Under the bridge, Lowdown and Cal stood in the stream that fed the Deepwater. The water was cool and soothed Cal's damaged paw. By the time the others caught up with them it was bleeding less, but a shard of green glass was still embedded in the pad.

"Did they follow you?" he asked Tazar.

"No! We scared them good. The only danger is if they tell the Ruzelas. They'd love it: 'Wild Dogs Attack Innocent Uprights.' It'd give them a great excuse to come looking for us."

"I know," said Cal miserably. "We're going to have to lay low for a couple of days."

His ears and tail drooped with guilt. He'd broken every rule, and he knew it. Never swipe food directly from humans, but wait until they leave it or throw it away; never challenge humans on their own ground, but retreat, reassemble, and rethink your plan; most important of all, never do anything without telling your brothers and sisters what you're going to do, and always make sure that they're prepared for anything that might happen. What with the pain and the guilt, he felt really sick. He turned to his leader.

"Tazar, back there, you know, I, well . . ."

"Stow it, Cal. I've been that hungry, too," Tazar said.

"I wasn't even really hungry. I mean, we ate yesterday, but that sausage smelled so good. I wanted it more than anything in the world."

"I know," said Tazar. "We haven't been eating too well lately. Still," he added cheerfully, thumping his tail against Waggit's back, "our little brother here got his first blood today, in a manner of speaking. Maybe his second'll be killing a nice fat scurry, but what we've got to do now is get that paw fixed and get you back to the tunnel."

Waggit watched as Raz gently took hold of the loose skin at the back of Cal's neck, and held it firmly in his mouth. Then Cal held up his paw, and Lowdown carefully took hold of the shard of glass between his front teeth. There was a soft yelp as the little dog pulled it out and spat it in the water. Tazar came around, and while Cal held up his paw the leader licked it with his large, pink tongue. After a while he stopped and looked at Waggit.

"Come here and lick your brother's wound," he ordered.

"Me?" said Waggit. "Lick?"

"Sure, it's good for it. It has healing powers," said Tazar.

So Waggit did as he was told. He could feel the roughness of the pad on his tongue, and taste the saltiness of the blood in his mouth. Tazar inspected the wound with all the pomposity of a doctor and proclaimed it good enough. Cal then splashed his way to the mud on the bank and buried his foot in the softest part to seal the cut and stop the bleeding.

Tazar's main concern now was to organize their safe return to the tunnel. There were two problems. The first they faced every day, which was that five dogs without an owner were seen as a threat. The other problem was that they had lost their greatest advantage—speed. Therefore their route had to be through the most densely wooded and least-used parts of the park. Where cutting across open ground was unavoidable, it was to be done as swiftly as possible, one by one, each dog waiting on the other side until they were all together again.

"Okay," said Tazar, in his busiest organizing tones, "who's got the best eyes?"

Lowdown chuckled a wheezing laugh. "Not me,

boss, that's fer sure. Mine are getting so bad that pretty soon I'm going to need my own petulant to guide me."

"Well, I guess it's down to Raz and Waggit. Raz, you take the nose and Waggit the tail."

What this meant, Tazar explained, was that Raz would be the lead dog, going ahead to scout out each section of the route, while Waggit would stay at the rear to make sure there was no attack from behind.

The going was hard because of the route they were forced to take, the brush catching in coats already thickening with the onset of winter, and briars scratching the soft skin of the dogs' stomachs. Waggit was filled with a strange mixture of apprehension, pride, and fear. It felt very good to have been given such an important job, but the lives of the dogs might very well depend on him doing it properly, and this was frightening. No less frightening was the realization that, if there were an attack from behind, he would be the first one the attackers would hit.

In fact it turned out that the greatest danger came from his own determination to do the job properly. He spent so much time looking over his shoulder that he was almost left behind on several occasions. The sound of him crashing through the undergrowth in a panicky attempt to catch up should have alerted every ranger in the park, but all it actually did was scare a lot of small animals and earn him disapproving looks from Tazar.

The most difficult part of the journey was by the side of the Bigwater. The deeply wooded area they were in came to an end, and the dogs needed to cross a grassy meadow and the horse path before they would reach the safety of another thin line of trees. Then more open ground would have to be faced before they reached the woods again.

Raz went first, walking determinedly toward the tree line. He made it without incident, and his body all but disappeared in the thickest part of the undergrowth. They gave him a few more minutes before Cal, flanked by Tazar on one side and Lowdown on the other, set off on the same route, trying to conceal the fact that Cal was injured as much as possible.

Waggit was alone now and just plain scared. He knew that he mustn't start out too soon, but the waiting was agony. Every sound of the woods caused him to start, and the sighing of the wind in the branches seemed to be the whispering of hidden enemies. He could stand it no longer and moved out.

Halfway between the woods and the tree line he saw it: a ranger on a horse, by Lowdown's estimation the most dangerous kind of human. The ranger appeared not to have seen him yet. Waggit knew that he should keep to the rules and walk, but he seemed to have lost control of his legs as they broke into a run by themselves. When he got to the tree line he kept to the far side so that it was between him and the ranger, who passed by without realizing the terror he was striking into the puppy's heart.

At the end of the tree line Waggit paused for a moment. It was open ground from there to the safety of the woods some distance away. There was no choice but to gather up the last remaining shreds of courage and go forward. His path took him past a large old tree, and as he rounded its far side an equally large old man came out from behind it. The two nearly bumped into each other. The man looked at him, bent down, and held out his hand.

"Hello little doggie, doggie. Where are you going?" he said.

Waggit looked straight ahead and walked firmly toward his destination. The man, his friendship rejected, lost interest and went off in the other direction. Only a day before, the young dog would have sniffed the offered hand, wagged his tail, and been eager to please this stranger, but now he remembered the angry men with their sticks and kept his distance. He was learning the difficult lessons of survival.

The others were waiting for him when he got to the woods. From now on the journey was much safer, which was fortunate, because the loss of blood and the pain had drained Cal of his energy, and this last part was much more difficult for him than the others. It was a great relief for all of them when their sanctuary was in sight.

Waggit was surprised at how glad he was to be home, surprised that he felt he *was* home, even more surprised when he realized that he hadn't thought of his master once since the events at the Skyline End.

Only the Lady Alicia was in the tunnel as they filed in. She had obviously been asleep. She got up and shook herself, and noticed that everyone's attention was directed toward Cal.

"What's the matter with him?" she said sulkily.

Nobody answered her. They weren't deliberately ignoring her, but everyone was so busy helping Cal to lie down in his box, and covering him in newspaper and cardboard, that they all assumed somebody else would reply. This assumption was shattered into a thousand pieces by her shriek of anger.

"Don't anyone around here talk to me no more? What am I, just decoration?"

Although she was closer to the truth than she knew, Tazar tried to calm her down with his most soothing voice.

"It's nothing to worry about, my lady. Brother Cal's just become the latest victim of the Upright's inability to live with any creature he can't lord it over. Cal's cut his paw. It's bad, but it's not serious."

"Oh yeah?" she said with little interest. "What was he doing?"

"He was trying to get us a nice, fat sausage for our supper."

"Oh, great!" She yawned again. "I'm starved."

"Well, unfortunately, dear princess, the sausage remains with its original owner," muttered Tazar, "probably at this moment in his great fat stomach."

"No sausage! Oh dear, Tazie! Well, what else didja get?" She rubbed her body up against his.

"As of now, not a lot. We spent the whole time

getting Cal back here safely."

"And what food did *you* manage to get, Alicia?" asked Raz, who was offended by her indifference to his best friend's injury.

"Nothing yet. I was just going out as you came in."

"So early in the day!" Raz said sarcastically. "Don't overtire yourself, honey."

"Listen, wise guy, dogs who are as highly bred as me are very delicate and need more rest, which probably accounts for *your* endless energy."

The prospect of a whole day without a meal worried Tazar. If the dogs didn't eat they got irritable, often fighting with one another, and their general morale went down. Worse, if they weren't eating as a group, it encouraged the younger dogs to go off to fend for themselves, which weakened the idea of acting as a team.

"Where's everyone else?" Tazar demanded. "What's happened to Magica and Gordo?"

"You know those two," answered Alicia, "probably cavorting in the woods, getting all messed up."

"And Gruff?" Tazar asked.

"He's on the bridge. He said he'd be eyes and ears for a while so's I wouldn't be disturbed. I'm surprised you didn't see him when you came in," said Alicia.

"So'm I," said Tazar. "We could've been Tashi's team and a mob of Stoners for all the warning he gave."

"You're right!" Gruff's lack of protection of her person was gradually dawning on Alicia. "I could've been attacked in my own home."

"What're we going to do, boss? We should eat today." Lowdown knew and shared Tazar's worries. "It's getting late. What with the Skurdies and loners, there ain't going to be much left in the trash cans."

The small dog was right, and the leader knew it. One of the disadvantages of living on the Risingside, with its greater space that provided more hiding places and safe spots, was the presence of loners, dogs who depleted the area's already sparse and scattered food supply. It seemed to Tazar that there was only one thing to do.

"We have no choice. As soon as it gets dark, we nighthunt!"

4

The Nighthunt

It promised to be a good night for hunting. The early autumn evening was clear and crisp, and even though sound and smell are in many ways more important to dogs than sight, the bright moonlight would help them see any animal that broke cover and tried to make a run for it. There was an air of excitement in the tunnel as each dog anticipated the night's adventures. Gordo and Raz were discussing whether they preferred to eat mice, rats, squirrels, or rabbits, or, in team language, nibblers, scurries, curlytails, and hoppers.

Gordo, whose favorite subject was food, was of the opinion that hoppers were the best, but that you hardly ever got one. He thought curlytails were sweeter eating than scurries, while Raz felt that nibblers were too small and too bony to be worth the bother. Gruff, overhearing the conversation, said, "Personally I don't like fresh meat. I find it hard to digest, and it gives me gas. I'll take a nice ham sandwich any day."

"Not this day, you won't," said Tazar. "There'll be nothing to eat if we don't hunt."

Waggit had never eaten raw meat in his short life, and had no idea what would taste best. Up until two days ago his food had come from a can opened by his owner and scooped into a bowl. He had never had a problem with this system and was worried about adapting to the new situation. Furthermore he wasn't quite sure what he would be expected to do, and more than ever he wished that his owner would come to rescue him and take him back to where the meals were regular and the demands put upon a puppy were few.

Tazar began to organize the team prior to their departure.

"Lady Alicia, Cal, Gordo, and Lowdown, you'll all stay here and guard the tunnel."

"Aw, boss!" Lowdown said in protest. This was the second time today that he had been left behind to be a caretaker. "Why can't I come with the hunting party?"

"I need you here," Tazar said in his most serious and important voice. "This is our home, the most valuable thing we have, and someone of your intelligence must guard it. If Tashi's mob has a spy out there who sees us all leave, they may very well try to take it over."

"So it's got nothing to do with my short legs and lack of speed?"

"Absolutely not. That's the furthest thing from my mind," said Tazar.

"You think they'd attack?" asked Gordo, nervous of having to fight for the right to stay in his own cozy bed.

"Don't worry," retorted Lowdown. "If they do you just have to lie on 'em and they'll soon give in. Fortunately it don't take a whole lot of brains." His last remark was directed more toward Tazar than Gordo. He was still upset at being left behind.

Tazar ignored this and lined up the remaining dogs. "Lady Magica, you hunt with Raz, and Waggit and I will work together. If we see a likely target we'll split up, you two attacking from one side and we'll attack from the other. Because Waggit and Magica are the fastest they should try and get ahead of any prey and drive it toward Raz and me for the kill. If it's a curly-tail make sure it doesn't get up a tree. That's how we always lose them."

While Waggit was glad to hear from these instructions that he wasn't expected to actually kill anything, they still sounded complicated to his puppy brain. Which side would they attack from, and how would he get ahead of whatever it was they were attacking? How did you drive something in a direction it didn't want to go, anyway?

"Waggit, you'll do just fine." Lady Magica had been watching the frown on his face. "We work as a team, so if you make a mistake we cover it for you. Nobody expects you to be a hero the first time out."

While her kindness gave him some comfort, he was anxious as they prepared to move out into the stillness of the park at night. Before they left, Tazar stood in front of an old movie poster that was stuck to the wall. It had been there longer than any of them could remember, and showed a fierce-looking dog with its fangs bared, staring directly and menacingly out. It had faded to muted colors, with long streaks from where water had run down it, but it was still a powerful image. Tazar looked up at it with reverence, for team legend had it that it was the face of Vinda the Powerful, a mystical being upon whose favor success depended.

"Great Vinda, give us good fortune on our hunt tonight, and protect our brothers and sisters," he chanted. The dogs gave soft howls in response, and the hunting party moved out of the tunnel.

When they had cleared the bushes that surrounded the entrance and had emerged into the open, Waggit noticed the way the other dogs lowered their bodies close to the ground as they went forward, taking long, slow steps, ears pricked and noses twitching. He tried to do the same, but it seemed awkward, and he caught his foot under a tree root. He yelped in pain, breaking the silence that was so important if the hunt was to be successful, and so he resumed his normal walk. Then a strange thing happened—he'd gone only a short distance when he realized that he was moving just like the others were. The gait came naturally if you didn't think about it, and with it you could move noiselessly through the park.

At first it seemed that they were the only animals

around. They moved up to a wide path that cut across the park, which the team called the Crossway. Humans used it as a shortcut, but for the dogs it marked the boundary between the Skyline End and the Deepwoods, where the paths were narrower, the bushes thicker, and the trees much closer together. Waggit had never been in this part of the park, and he couldn't see how you could chase anything through it, because the undergrowth was so dense. If he were somebody's prey it would be exactly the sort of place he would choose to live. Which, of course, was why Tazar had brought the party there; he knew that it was an area full of the small rodents that were the dogs' main food source in hard times.

The hunters followed their leader into the Deepwoods until they came upon two paths, narrow but negotiable, that ran almost parallel to each other. In silent communication Raz and Magica took the right-hand path, while Tazar veered to the left, followed by a nervous Waggit. As soon as they entered the wooded area they could hear the rustling sound of their would-be suppers escaping. Suddenly Magica leapt forward and plunged into the undergrowth, her powerful legs propelling her in great leaps over the low-growing bushes and through the clumps of trees. Without thinking Waggit ran forward down the path he and Tazar had taken, instinctively trying to get ahead of whatever it was she pursued. Suddenly she stopped dead and looked up at one of the trees. Waggit saw a squirrel scamper up its trunk and through the branches, leaping from the higher ones to the next tree until it was out of sight. By this time Tazar had caught up with him, slightly out of breath.

"Curlytails!" he said. "They're so hard to get before they reach a tree, and once they're up there, they're gone."

Magica had rejoined Raz on the other path, and all four moved on. Because of the commotion caused by the short chase it was several hundred yards before they heard any more movement. Three times in the next hour the dogs pursued various small creatures, only to have them escape into the undergrowth. By now they were near the far end of the park, where the landscape became more open.

As Waggit and Tazar rounded a corner the path opened up into a small glade. Waggit stopped and felt his hackles rising. There in front of him, no more than fifty feet away, was a fat squirrel sitting eating something. It had its back to Waggit, but every so often it would stop its nibbling, look around, and smell the air, its whiskers twitching as it tried to pick up the scent of danger. Fortunately the dogs were downwind of the animal, so it couldn't smell them.

To the left was a large rock. If he could reach it without detection, Waggit could use it as cover to skirt around and get ahead of his prey. From that position he could drive the squirrel toward Tazar.

Waggit slowly moved forward as Tazar got into position to receive the prey. Slinking so low that he could feel his belly dragging on the ground, Waggit inched quietly forward. He was within ten feet of his target when he stepped on a small stick that broke with a sound like a rifle shot in the still of the night. The squirrel whirled around, saw the danger it was in, and ran into the open glade. Waggit bounded after it at full speed. Now in the middle of the clearing, the squirrel started to run in a zigzag pattern, constantly changing direction, hoping to confuse its attacker. Waggit, who was easily confused, stopped, mesmerized by the performance. With a quick dash it tried to escape, but made a fatal error. When it should have fled into the woods, it went toward the rock, which was too steep and too slippery for the small animal to climb. There was nowhere it could go that Waggit couldn't grab it, and the squirrel knew it.

The two animals faced each other, neither quite sure what to do next. Waggit could smell the waves of fear coming off his prey, and suddenly the animal started chattering in high-pitch panic. The dog looked into its eyes and realized that, although it was fat in preparation for the long, lean winter months ahead, it was young, like him, barely fully grown—another puppy, or whatever you called a young squirrel. He sat down, unable to make the final kill.

The squirrel grabbed its chance and ran along the foot of the rock and into the woods beyond. The whole drama had only taken a few seconds, but to Waggit it seemed like hours. He heard Tazar behind him and felt the leader's breath on the back of his neck.

With quiet anger the older dog said, "You let it go. You had it cornered and you let it go."

"I didn't know what to do. I've never done this before." A whimper came into the puppy's voice.

"What you do is kill it," Tazar said sternly. "The rules are different now. These are the rules of survival;

not just your survival, but that of your brothers and sisters."

"I don't have brothers and sisters. You're all just a bunch of dogs I ran into when I got lost," Waggit whined.

"They are your brothers and sisters in more ways than you know right now. That you will soon discover."

Waggit was so upset, and so longing for his owner to come back and rescue him, that he didn't even bother to ask Tazar what he meant.

The Lady Magica and Raz had caught up with them.

"Wassup?" asked Raz.

"Oh, nothing. Just another curlytail that got away," said Tazar. "I don't think we're going to get anything tonight. Let's go back home."

"Go home empty-mouthed?" Magica was incredulous. "You never do that!"

"Well tonight I am," Tazar shot back, irritably.

Magica and Raz looked at each other. "Ooookay," said Raz. "You're the boss, but it won't go down too well with Alicia. You know how she is on an empty stomach."

"Well, she doesn't have to put up with much, and

one day without food isn't the end of the world." And the black dog stalked off toward home.

"What's the matter with him?" Raz asked Waggit.

"He's mad at me because I let the curlytail get away," Waggit replied.

"Well, they can be very fast if you're not used to them," consoled Magica.

"No, it wasn't that," Waggit said. "I could've got it, but I let it go."

"Yup. That would make him mad, all right," sighed Raz. "Why didja do it?"

"It's an animal like you and me," said Waggit.

"No, not like you and me. It's a food animal, and that's the difference," said Raz.

Waggit didn't know what to say to this, so he said nothing. In silence the three of them made their way back to the tunnel. At night the dogs kept to the wide paths wherever possible. Without the presence of humans, the open ground was safer than the enclosed areas of the woods or narrow gullies, where an ambush by Tashi's team or even late-night Stoners was always a possibility. Waggit was surprised at how quickly they got back, and even more amazed to find that a full meal awaited them. Just like the night before, piles of food were laid out in a circle. Some of the piles had sausage, some had ham, and others had some rather old-looking and unidentifiable meat. Added to each pile were some very dry, stale bread rolls, but to the hungry dogs it was a banquet.

"Great Vinda!" exclaimed Raz. "Where did all this come from?"

"Lowdown," said Tazar, "did you have anything to do with this?"

"Aw, well, actually it was the Lady Alicia's idea in the first place," Lowdown said modestly.

"It was?" Alicia seemed surprised.

"Sure," said Lowdown. "Remember you said it was a pity that the Upright feeder was in Tashi's realm, because they were always throwing away good food?" The Upright feeder was a restaurant that was located in the park near the Deepwater.

"Yes," Alicia said, cautiously.

"And you remember you said that all our troubles would be over if someone could get near the place without being roughed up by Tashi's hooligans?" continued Lowdown.

"Yes, I said that."

"Well, that's what gave me the idea," said Lowdown.

"Yeah, you're right. It was my idea. See," she said, looking at Tazar, "I do get 'em sometimes!"

"However in this case, as in many," said the leader, "it wasn't so much the idea as the execution that was important."

"Yeah, but," Alicia replied, "he wasn't . . ."

"Wasn't what?"

"Executed." She was triumphant. "And Tashi would've if he'd caught him!"

The other team members stifled laughter at this.

"Tell us," Tazar said to Lowdown, still choking on laughter, "exactly what happened."

"Well, boss, I remembered that the feeder closes down soon, what with the cold days coming on and no Uprights wanting to go there. They always get rid of a lot of food in the big bins in the back just before they close. Anyway, I knows all this 'cause the same time last year Tashi's mob was boasting about how full of good food they was, and challenged us to come to their realm and try and take some, an offer we did refuse, if you remember."

"Go on, go on." Tazar clearly did not want to be reminded of unmet challenges. Plus, it was a constant source of irritation to him that the feeder was in

Tashi's realm and not his.

"We know that Tashi has eyes and ears all around the feeder," continued Lowdown, "but there's one weak spot—a place that he can't control—and that's the door where the Uprights go in. And what takes some of the Uprights there? Luggers pulled by longlegs. So Gordo and me worked out a plan. Where the road bends just before the feeder there's a big rock with bushes around it, big enough to hide Gordo from Tashi's mob."

"Hey," said Gordo, "I ain't that big."

"Whether you is or isn't ain't the point. The point is that you was able to hide there while I went up the road to the feeder."

Lady Magica, who was wide-eyed with excitement by now, asked, "But how did you get there without any of Tashi's team seeing you?"

"Smart, you see!" Lowdown had a big grin on his face. "I waited until a longlegs and a lugger came past the rock, then I ran out and got between the two big wheels at the back. If I walked at the same pace as the longlegs, which ain't difficult, let me tell you, the wheels hid me enough so that none of Tashi's boys could see me, and even if they did, what could they do? Are they going to attack a lugger full of Uprights? I don't think so."

"But how did you get to the food and bring it back?" asked Raz.

"I had to wait until the Uprights got out of the lugger and went into the feeder. Then the longlegs have to go past the big bins on their way out, so I dashes around the wheels over to the bins, pulls out some stuff, and wait until the next lugger comes around, and that takes me back the same way to where Gordo is hid. I leave what I've grabbed with him and take the next lugger back to the feeder. We did this about four times, which took a while. Then, of course, we had to drag the stuff back, which again took some time, and that, ladies and gentledogs, is how you got your supper."

There were general sighs of approval from the team at this tale of daring, sounds that were suddenly overwhelmed with the hearty noise of Gordo's stomach rumbling.

"I think Gordo's stomach has heard enough talk of food and is eager for the real thing, as are we all," said Tazar.

Once again, as on the night before, each dog sat before his or her assigned pile, and waited until their leader gave the same invocation:

"Remember as you eat, you eat your brother's food; remember as you sleep, you take your sister's space; remember as you live, your life belongs to them. You are the team; the team is you. The two are one; the one is two."

There was much more food than last night, and the silence was interrupted only by the sounds of chewing and lips smacking, plus the occasional belch. Hunting, or, more accurately, chasing, had given Waggit a fierce appetite, and he eagerly attacked the pile in front of him. Even the stale bread roll tasted good. It didn't take long for them all to finish, and then there was a lot of stretching, scratching, and yawning, and general signs of satisfaction. Soon the dogs started to move to their boxes and began settling down for the night. One of the team had dragged a new box into the tunnel for Waggit and layered the bottom with fresh newspaper. It looked comfortable and smelled good, but just as he was turning around and around in preparation for lying down, a terrifying howl shattered the still night air.

The dogs leapt up, all thoughts of sleep vanished, and they ran to the mouth of the tunnel. In the distance, on a rock outcrop, two dogs stood. One was strong—not big, but tightly muscled—with short hair and pointy ears, and this was Tashi. Next to him was Wilbur—a nasty, sly-looking animal, with wiry, matted fur and an obsequious look—known to the Tazarians as Tashi's "evil lieutenant."

"Tazar, you wretch," the tough dog bellowed, "listen to me, Tashi, the ruler of this park. Your curs have transgressed. They invaded my realm and stole our food. You and those miserable mutts will pay for this. There will be a battle to end all battles, but it will be at a time and place of my choosing. Until then, make peace with your god, for you will meet him very soon."

As suddenly as they had appeared they disappeared, leaving a hush over the Tazarians. They looked in silence toward their leader, who brought himself up to his full height, and in a quiet, confident voice, said, "We knew it must come to this. We are prepared; let them do their worst."

5

Tashi's Challenge

As the days passed, life as a team member became easier for Waggit. He grew more familiar with the park, especially the location of its danger zones and safe shelters. He now knew where there were too many people, which routes the park rangers took, where Tashi's realm began, and also the safest spots for swimming, the best vantage points for looking, and the places where you could take a nap in the afternoon if you suddenly felt sleepy and were far from the tunnel. The early fall weather was unusually warm, which meant that people were still having their lunches in the park and leaving behind enough food to feed an army of Waggits, and he was becoming familiar with which spots yielded the best fare. Of course he continued to hope that he would find his owner and spent many hours watching the place where they had become separated.

The dog with whom he had become most friendly was Lowdown. There was no doubt in Waggit's mind that his short, scruffy friend was the shrewdest dog he had ever met. What he lacked in looks he made up for in smarts. Sometimes he was so perceptive that Waggit thought he possessed magical powers. He could tell which route a ranger would take, or what Tazar's mood would be when he got home, or when a storm would happen. This last ability was especially important to Waggit, who was terrified of thunder and lightning.

Lowdown also loved to have fun. He particularly enjoyed playing practical jokes, especially on Waggit. One day they were in an unfamiliar part of the park. It was about midway between the Deepwoods and the Skyline End, and the dogs had to go very carefully, for it was an area where people brought their children to play. The little ones saw more than the grown-ups and could often spot an animal in the bushes that their parents would miss. This area also marked the boundary of Tashi's realm, where he regularly posted members of his team on eyes-and-ears duty.

It was not surprising, therefore, when Lowdown suddenly growled, "Quick, down!" Waggit instantly sprawled onto his stomach, his legs splayed. He was so flat to the ground that he looked as if he had been dropped from the sky.

"Don't look up," said Lowdown.

Looking up was the last thing on Waggit's mind, and he began to take an intense interest in some rather fascinating dead leaves in front of his nose.

"It's one of Tashi's team."

The leaves became more and more interesting every time Lowdown opened his mouth.

"Here's what we should do," Lowdown said after a few moments' thought. "I'll go out and confront him. While the two of us are staring each other out, you make your way behind him and pounce on his back."

"W-w-w-why can't I do the staring bit? I think I would be good at that," whispered Waggit.

"Because if *I* leapt on his back he wouldn't even

notice," the little dog said in a hushed voice.

"Okay, then." Waggit was resigned to his fate. Then a brilliant idea struck him. "Why don't we just run away?"

"Oh, he'd love that. He'd love to chase us. He'd probably invite all his friends. Plus, I wouldn't like to be the one to explain to Tazar why two of us couldn't take on one Tashini, would you?"

The answer to the question was no—even to a dog who had known the leader for only a few days. So Lowdown moved out from the cover of the bushes, stood squarely on the path, growled, and fixed the enemy with an intense stare. Waggit lifted his head and saw their opponent for the first time. He was a large dog, bigger than Waggit had hoped, with a coat of an unusual color, almost golden and very glossy. He stood rigidly, returning Lowdown's stare, and would continue to do so until one of them broke eye contact, thereby acknowledging the other's superiority. Since Lowdown acknowledged nobody's superiority except Tazar's, Waggit knew this could go on for some time.

He crawled as quietly as he could for one who was trembling with fear, until he was poised on a rock behind and above his target. He got ready to spring onto the other dog's back, although what he would do next he had no idea. The Tashini had not moved.

Suddenly Waggit was in the air. Where he got the courage to make the leap he didn't know, but there he was, on his way down in what he hoped was a fearsome attack stance. He landed on the back of the dog with a bang that temporarily knocked the wind out of him and caused a ringing in his ears. He quickly realized, however, that it was not in his ears but was coming from the dog's body, which was hard, cold, and smelled of metal. The animal hadn't moved one inch but was still staring at Lowdown, or would have been had the scruffy little dog not been lying on his back, literally howling with laughter.

Waggit looked around and realized that the animal upon whose back he now perched wasn't real at all. It was a metal statue of a dog, which was why its coat had such a strange color and shine. He also realized that he was the victim of one of Lowdown's practical jokes, part of the entertainment for the day.

And entertained Lowdown certainly was, rolling around on his back, his legs scratching the air with glee.

"Oh, Dear Vinda, that was good," he wheezed. "You

certainly fell for that one. Oh, bless my fleas, you scared the life out of him. He's gone rigid with fear!"

"Oh, very funny," said Waggit. "I suppose this'll be the talk of the tunnel tonight."

"You can count on it," the prankster replied.

From the back of the metal dog, Waggit could see some distance along the path. Suddenly his ears pricked, and the hackles on his back rose in fear.

"Lowdown, two dogs coming, and they're not petulants. They could be Tashinis."

"Sure there are." Lowdown was still laughing. "An army of them, I wouldn't be surprised!"

"No, seriously, there are. Take a look around that bush."

The alarm in Waggit's voice sounded real, and it was enough to make Lowdown stop laughing and peer around a large bush that bordered the path. What he saw made him bark urgently to Waggit. "It's Spotty the Executioner and Tommy Teeth. Get down off that stupid metal monster now; we've got to go."

Without pausing to think what a silly name Spotty was for an executioner, Waggit half fell, half leapt down from the statue, tumbling to the ground. As soon as he landed they both took off at full speed through the woods, neither one of them the least concerned about what Tazar would say if he knew they had fled from Tashinis.

When they reached a small clearing, Lowdown, whose wind was never good at the best of times, collapsed, panting and making little whistling noises as he breathed.

"Thank Vinda you was up there and saw them," he said when he could talk again. "Those two are the meanest, most vicious of all the Tashinis. If they'd have got us it would've been bye-bye, Waggit, and bye-bye, Lowdown, believe me."

Waggit saw no reason not to.

When Lowdown's breathing had fully returned to normal, they left the glade at a more dignified pace, and after a time Waggit felt almost excited about their narrow escape. Surviving danger made life seem awfully good. Everything appeared sharper and clearer; even the air smelled different. Waggit sensed that Lowdown felt it, too, as the dogs reached the safety of the Risingside and Tazar's realm. It was good to be two friends trotting along with the sun on their backs, feeling the crunch of newly fallen leaves beneath their paws.

❦ ❦ ❦

There were only two clouds casting gloom on the team. One was Tashi's warning of revenge. From experience they knew that Tashi and his evil lieutenant, Wilbur, would make good on the threat, probably when the Tazarians least expected it. The dogs couldn't afford to relax and be off-guard for one moment with this hanging over them, which put a considerable strain on them all. Eyes-and-ears duty at night was particularly stressful, as each bush that moved in the wind seemed to take on the form of an enemy preparing for attack.

What made the situation even more nerve-racking was the fact that Tazar had declared that the next encounter with the Tashinis would be the last. He was tired of the hostilities that kept flaring up, disrupting the life of the team. Furthermore Tazar passionately believed that all of the dogs in the park should concentrate their energies against the common enemy— humans. He thought it was a waste of time fighting one another when they could all be concentrating on stealing food, keeping an eye on the rangers, or camouflaging their shelters.

So Tazar was determined that the next battle with

the Tashinis would be one of such ferocity that the victorious team would become the sole rulers of the entire park. It was not something to which the Tazarians were looking forward, for Tashi had some fearsome fighters. Spotty the Executioner and Tommy Teeth were just two of them.

The other dark spot was Waggit's inability to hunt, despite his natural attributes of speed and lightning-fast reactions. This certainly wasn't as big a problem as the impending hostilities with the rival team. In fact the unseasonably warm weather meant that it wasn't a problem at all at the moment, but each dog knew that when the colder days came the human leftovers would all but disappear. At that point there would be only two alternatives for food. One was to forage outside the confines of the park, which was extremely dangerous because there was the constant possibility of getting run over by cars or caught by the authorities. The second food source, and the one that they relied upon, was hunting. Even this was far from easy, because many a possible meal went to ground during the cold days, sleeping until warmth brought them back out of their holes and burrows. Those that were around seemed to be faster and sharper when it was cold, and more difficult to catch. Although the team had some capable hunters, they didn't have anyone with the natural abilities they could see in Waggit. It was frustrating, therefore, when he cornered an animal and then let it go, as he had done both times they had taken him hunting.

Tazar thought he understood the problem. Waggit still thought his former "owner" would rescue him, and because of this he didn't truly believe that his survival in the hard months ahead depended upon hunting. If he assumed he was about to return to a life where food was regularly delivered out of little metal cans, why should he kill to eat?

Tazar was a smart dog and a wise leader, and he knew that it would be pointless to confront the puppy face-to-face. Waggit wouldn't admit in front of the other dogs that he still secretly cherished thoughts of his master. No, there was a better way to convince him that there would be no rescue, that he had been abandoned, and that, like it or not, his survival was now and forever linked with that of the team. Tazar would do it tonight.

That evening they had a fine dinner, consisting mainly of hot dogs. Lady Magica had found a large pack of these delicacies tossed in a garbage can. Apart from the green furry bits, they were in perfect condition, and Gordo even insisted that their newly grown fuzz added to the flavor and protected you from the cold. When they had finished and were still in a circle, Tazar called them to attention.

"My brothers and sisters," he said in his best booming tones, "it occurred to me that, since we have a new brother in our midst"—he nodded toward Waggit, who sat next to him—"it would help him get to know and understand us better if we each told the stories of how we came to be here. Magica, provider of tonight's good bounty, maybe you would care to get the ball rolling?"

At the sound of the word "ball" Gordo, who had been nodding off, suddenly sat upright with his ears pricked—once a retriever, always a retriever.

Lady Magica looked down, took a deep breath, and started.

"Sure, Tazar, I don't mind telling my story. I've been here for many risings, more than I can remember, really. But I used to live with Uprights, a man and a woman in a house with dirt outside that I could run around in, and it was nice. I got food every day, and the man would comb my coat and take me for walks. I always felt that he liked me more than the woman did, so I suppose I stayed closer to him and was pleased to see him more than her. It's only canine nature, isn't it? You take care of them that take care of you. They seemed okay for Uprights, but then things started to change. They would shout terrible sounds at each other all the time. What they were saying I have no idea, because I was young and never learned more than a few words of Upright, but you could feel the anger in the air. It nearly always ended up with the man walking out, and those were the worst times. When he had gone she used to shout at me and kick me, like I was him and it was me she was angry at. I soon got to know that I had to hide when he left."

Magica hesitated as if troubled by the memory. "This went on for some time," she continued after a minute or so, "and then one day she was very nice to me. She stroked me and gave me cookies, and asked me if I wanted to go for a walk. 'Walk' was one of the Upright words I did know. She put me on my leash. We got into the roller and drove for a long time. She finally stopped at a place I didn't know and walked me here, to the park. When we got here she looked around to see if there were any other Uprights watching, and then took off my leash and started beating me with it and kicking me, so I ran off to get away from her. I hid for a while, and then came back to see if she was still there, but she had gone. I knew then what she had done. She figured that the man loved me, and would be upset if I wasn't there, so to get back at him for all the things he'd shouted at her she left me here, a long way from home." She paused. "I bet he *was* upset, too."

The team was hushed. The story, which, apart from Waggit, they'd all heard before, still had the power to silence them. Tazar let the stillness hang over the group for a while. He then turned to Lowdown, who sat next to Magica in the circle.

"Lowdown?"

"Well, boss, so far as I know I ain't ever lived with Uprights. I know my old memory's not the most reliable, but I'm pretty certain about that. I do remember being with a dog that I think was my mom, living in a box at the back of a big building someplace, where exactly, who knows? Anyway, the Ruzelas came and took us to this sort of lockup where there were hundreds of other dogs, all stuck in these metal cages.

They put me in one and my mom in another, and there we stayed. It was horrible. The food was bad—made the green furry bits on tonight's dinner seem like a luxury—and we only got taken out of the cages once a day to take a couple of steps around a concrete yard, so if I've got short legs it ain't because of too much exercise as a youth." The team chuckled at this. One thing they all liked about Lowdown was his ability to see humor in even the grimmest situation. "If you was in this lockup, two things would happen to you. Uprights would come in every day, and if they liked the look of you they would take you away to live with them. Those that didn't get picked stayed in the cages for a while and then one of the Uprights that worked in the place would come and take you away and you'd never be seen again. Nobody knew exactly what happened to those that was taken, but we had a pretty good idea. Every time they came for one of us the rest would bark and howl, they was all so upset. Anyway, I'd been there a while. No surprise that no Upright picked me. After all I ain't decorative, am I? Then one night one of the women Uprights who was nicer than the others, always sneaking in bits of food and stuff for us, she came, opened the cage, and hid me under her coat. She kept me hidden until we got out of the building and down to the park, and then she put me on the dirt and said something that I didn't understand. I knew she was kind, and she was trying to help me, so I rubbed myself against her to show that I liked her, but she kept shooing me away. She had water coming out of her eyes, like Uprights do sometimes when they're upset. I think she knew that something bad would happen to me if I stayed in the lockup any longer, 'cause they had taken my mom away that same day, and I never saw her again."

And so they went on, each dog's story one of sadness and abandonment. Even Alicia could make you feel sorry for her when she told of being tied up to a tree with a rope that she had to chew through to get free. She spoiled the emotion of the moment, however, by shrieking, "I don't get it. I mean it's not like I'm made of spare parts or anything. I'm a purebred. Why would anyone want to abandon me?"

As each of the animals spoke Waggit felt as if layers of ice were forming around his heart. He became numb with sorrow, but the worst moment for him was when Cal told how he became a Tazarian.

"I was living with two Uprights in one of those big

buildings where lots of them live. Our part of it was small, but I prefer it that way. It's more cozy and friendly. Anyway, things were going along just swell until the little Upright came along. I actually liked him. He made a lot of noise, which I always wanted to do but wasn't allowed to. He also smelled great. I loved his scent. It was clean and nice. One day I was next to him and I licked him to find out if he tasted as good as he smelled, and the man went crazy. He smacked me across the nose and shouted at me and locked me in one of the small rooms. The next day I thought he'd forgotten all about it, and sure enough he seemed okay and took me for a walk here in the park. He even threw sticks for me, which was great because he didn't do it that often. He threw one that went a long way. It fell in bushes, and it took me some time to find. When I got it I went back to where the man had been, but he'd gone. I kept thinking he'd come back for me, but he never did."

Waggit couldn't believe his ears. What had happened to Cal was almost exactly what had happened to him. His owners had gotten a baby Upright, and although he hadn't ever licked it, the woman kept on shouting at him whenever he got near it. This went on for several days and it was clear that his master was distressed by what was happening. Waggit assumed that his master had taken him to the park, something that he'd never done before, to get him out of the house and let the woman calm down. Before that day he'd never thrown a ball for Waggit either. He'd thrown a ball a long way down a hill, and by the time Waggit had returned with it he had disappeared. Could it be that he had really been abandoned like all the others? Was it possible that his owner would never come back, and that he would live the rest of his life with the Tazarians? He liked the team, but then he liked his master, too, and life with him seemed a lot easier than life in the park. He stood up, feeling a little wobbly on his legs.

"I'm just going for a little walk," he said to nobody in particular.

Lowdown began to struggle to his feet to go with his young friend, but Tazar blocked his way.

"The boy needs to be alone," he growled softly. "Let him go. He'll be all right." And they both watched as Waggit disappeared into the black night.

6
Survival

By the time the dogs were getting ready to sleep, Waggit still hadn't returned. Lowdown was worried about him. The dog's stories had obviously upset him a lot, even though they'd achieved Tazar's intention of making him face up to the fact that he had been abandoned. Lowdown knew that in his present state of mind Waggit would be less alert to the dangers of the night, whether it was the Stoners or Tashi's team or even traffic.

"Boss," he asked Tazar, "do you think we should go

and look for Waggit?"

Cal and Raz overheard him.

"We could go," Cal volunteered. "We're good searchers, honest. Please let us go."

But Tazar was firm. "No," he said, "he needs time to come to terms with all that he's heard tonight. There's a risk that some harm could befall him, but it's a risk we'll have to take. Until he accepts his past he will never be comfortable with his future."

There were times when you could persuade Tazar to change his mind, and there were times when he was immovable, and the dogs recognized that there was no point pressing him on this any further. They sighed and settled down for the night as best they could. Lowdown found it difficult to sleep. He tossed and turned, scratched and snorted, and worried about Waggit until tiredness finally got the better of him and he drifted off into a sleep that was disturbed by dreams of terrifying monsters attacking puppies, and Stoners and Ruzelas, and storms with terrible thunder and lightning.

He awoke with a start several hours later as the dawn was breaking on a clear and much colder day. His alarm clock turned out to be Cal, gently nipping at his leg.

"Look who's here, Lowdown, and see what he's got."

The old dog blinked, yawned, and struggled to his feet. There at the entrance to the tunnel was Waggit, covered in mud and leaves. In his mouth he had a large, dead rabbit.

Tazar's instincts had been right once again. Knowing that his "owner" had discarded him like so much trash had a profound effect on Waggit. Now he knew that there would be no rescue, no cans of food. He hadn't wanted to kill the rabbit, but in doing so he was obeying the oldest law of the planet, that of survival.

Now he dropped the dead animal and entered the shelter that was his only home. He began to shake uncontrollably. Cal and Raz came to either side of him and pressed their bodies against his quivering form.

"It's okay," said Raz. "You get used to it. You get used to everything."

The change in Waggit was clear to everyone. He was more serious and focused, more suspicious, and less willing to take everything he was told at face value. Even his body language changed. He walked closer to the ground, never making eye contact with strangers, moving surreptitiously through the park, especially when he had to cross open terrain. He also lived up to Tazar's expectations of his abilities as a hunter, providing more food for the team than any other dog. When he went out on a hunt it was as if he shut down his emotions; he couldn't afford to feel sympathy for his prey, not anymore.

He was no longer an innocent puppy, but he was still a young dog, and he loved to do the things that young dogs do. This mostly meant wrestling with Cal and Raz, and occasionally with Lady Magica. If Lowdown was his soul mate, these three were his playmates. They would snarl and growl and roughhouse one another to the ground, teeth gnashing and lips curled. To the onlooker it was fearsome, but to the dogs it was harmless fun. When they regained enough breath they would move on to the next game. Sometimes they would play tug-of-war, with a dog on each end of a fallen branch, or chase stones down a hill, and they frequently ended up swimming in one of the more secluded parts of the Deepwater.

Lowdown and Gordo were content to watch these antics. The older dog couldn't participate because of his aches and pains; and, anyway, wrestling him to the ground would have been no challenge because he was so close to it to begin with. Pinning Gordo down, on the other hand, would have been a challenge for the combined efforts of the entire team. How he remained so enormous was one of the enduring mysteries of the park. At first the team suspected that he had a secret food source, but he didn't. It was just how he was built, and he stayed the same in good times and in bad, in sickness and in health.

Gordo refused to participate in the games for two reasons. The first was that he was afraid that he'd hurt someone by accident. The second, and to him the more important reason, was the pleasure that he got from watching the love of his life, Magica, play-fight with the boys and give as good as she got. If for some reason she wasn't part of the free-for-all he would generally nod off to sleep, his second favorite activity.

Another park mystery, along with Gordo's weight, was what Tazar did during the day. Sometimes he would hang out with the rest of the team, but it was more usual for him to leave by himself in the morning and return shortly before the meal in the evening, unless there was an emergency that he had to deal with. Lowdown told Waggit that he thought Tazar spent his days gathering intelligence about what was happening in the park. Indeed there was nothing that occurred within its boundaries that he didn't know about. He had a favorite saying—"There's no such thing as a pleasant surprise"—and to him, knowledge was control.

Tazar's obsession with knowledge saved two of the team members some days later. The pleasant, unusually warm weather had ended, and a brisk cold spell had taken its place, cold enough to make people take lunch where they worked, or in restaurants outside of the park. It was also chilly enough for the small animals that lived in the woods to stay in their warm holes beneath the earth. There was very little food and the dogs were hungry. Cal and Raz expended more energy than most of their teammates, and therefore needed more calories. They were on a foraging expedition that took them close to those places most frequented by humans, in the vague hope that some of the hardier ones would still be taking a quick lunch on a bench. Cal's nose suddenly quivered.

He turned to Raz and said, "Do you smell what I smell, brother?"

Cal lifted his snout and took several sharp intakes of breath. "I do indeed, brother—meat, and not too far away by the smell of it."

The two of them moved forward in silence, their nostrils flared and twitching. Suddenly they came upon a strange wire structure, in the middle of which was a slab of red, delicious, fragrant meat.

"Oh my," said Cal.

"Indeed," said Raz.

Then they saw that no more than twenty feet away was a similar enclosure with an equally attractive meal lying inside. Cal's stomach growled in appreciation.

"You take this one," he said to Raz, nodding to the closer of the two, "and I'll take the other." Just as they were going to snap up their finds they heard a familiar bark behind them. They whirled around to see Tazar imperiously perched on a rock.

"I would think twice before doing that if I were either one of you," he said.

"But why, boss?" asked Cal, with just the hint of a whine in his voice. "It smells like good meat."

"I'm sure it's the best the Ruzelas could find," Tazar agreed.

"But why would the Ruzelas leave meat in the

woods?" asked Raz, genuinely confused.

"Well, first of all, let me say this," said Tazar. "Whenever you find something that seems strange, be very, very suspicious. Have you ever seen these wire dens before?"

"Well, no," the other two agreed.

"Now let me answer your question with action rather than words."

Tazar looked around until he found a long, straight, dead branch, one end of which he grasped in his mouth. Then he ran with it toward the meat in the cage. When the far end struck the food, a spring-loaded door came crashing down, sealing off the entrance, and therefore the exit, for any animal trapped inside. Cal and Raz both gasped.

Tazar dropped the branch.

"I saw the Ruzelas setting up these devices earlier this morning. Get caught in one of these little beauties and you end up in the Great Unknown."

"However . . ." Tazar chuckled, a wicked smile upon his face. "It *is* nice of the Ruzelas to leave out food for us, especially in these lean times. Cal, get ready," he commanded.

Cal got ready, for what he had no idea. But he was

prepared for anything that Tazar wanted him to do. The branch was still stuck in the mouth of the cage. Because the branch was curved, there was a gap between the door and the ground. Tazar maneuvered his powerful body into this space and began to push upward with all his might to force open the door. But it wouldn't budge.

"Get over here and help me," he panted to Raz. The dog ran over and put his weight underneath the door as well, and between them they managed to force it open no more than six inches. For Cal, however, this was more than enough space to crawl through and retrieve the meat with a howl of triumph.

"Let's do the other one, too," he said excitedly.

The two dogs scurried into the woods and soon came back with another branch of a similar shape and length.

"Give it to me," Tazar ordered. "We'll do this one a little differently."

He put the branch in his mouth, but instead of springing the trap by touching the meat, he very carefully placed the tip of the branch in the far corner of the cage. Using only his teeth, he forced the branch against the top part of the hole where the trapdoor slid down. Seeing that the door was now jammed, Cal enthusiastically ran in to get the meat.

There was a crack, followed by a clang as the branch snapped in two and the door slammed into place. Cal stood, with the meat in his mouth, inside the cage, with no apparent way of getting out.

"Oh no, Cal," said Raz. "Don't get trapped; don't let the Ruzelas get you. Please!"

Cal just stood there, still holding on to the meat, bewildered.

"Stupid. Stupid. Stupid. I was so stupid," said Tazar, the anger clear in his voice. "We should have quit when we were ahead. What are we going to do about this?"

He thought for a moment.

"I need rocks, lots of rocks of all different sizes," he said.

Both he and Raz went about getting an assortment and bringing them to the front of the cage. The smaller ones they carried in their mouths, but the larger ones had to be rolled forward with their noses. When they had acquired what the leader considered to be enough he turned to Raz.

"What we are going to do is this," he said. "I'm going

to grab hold of the bottom of the trapdoor with my teeth and try and pull it up a little way. When I do, you push one of the small rocks underneath to stop it from going back down again. Then I'll try and pull it up a bit farther, and you push in a bigger rock, and so on until we make an opening big enough for Cal to crawl out."

"Okay, Tazar, let's do it," said Raz, desperate to get his friend free. Tazar hooked his big, curved bottom teeth around the wire of the door. He pulled as hard as he could. He felt the pressure in his mouth, but nothing moved. He uncoupled himself from the cage and looked at it, and then he spotted the problem. At the bottom there was a small latch that fell into position when the door came down. Very carefully he hooked a claw around the latch and pulled. A sharp stab of pain went up his leg as the pressure on his claw increased, but the latch clicked open.

"Okay," he said. "Let's try again."

This time both Tazar from the outside and Cal from the inside hooked their teeth through the wire. Raz counted to three, and the two dogs pulled with all their might. The spring was very strong, but the door moved up slightly. As it rose Raz quickly nudged a stone under it to prevent it from coming back down.

The other two released their grip, rested for a second, and then they all repeated the process, only this time Raz used a larger stone. They did this until he had put the largest stone, actually a good-size rock, under the door, which made a space just big enough for Cal to crawl through.

Cal started to position himself for his escape, then stopped and went back for the meat.

"Leave the meat," ordered Tazar. "You're more important than any meat."

"With all due respect, Tazar," said Cal, "I'm not going through all this to come out empty-mouthed."

He grabbed the meat and, keeping close to the ground, very slowly crawled to freedom. The three dogs were joyfully reunited. They ran back to the tunnel, prizes proudly held in their mouths.

That night the team feasted on good, fresh meat, and listened in awe to Cal's stories of how he had escaped certain death at the hands of the Ruzelas. The rest of the team said how brave he was, while Tazar and Raz, who had seen his frightened face and therefore knew otherwise, kept quiet.

7

The Cold White

The cold spell continued and got worse. The last of the leaves fell from the trees, and the sun was hidden for days on end by a thick blanket of dark gray clouds. The dogs felt their coats thickening around them as their bodies prepared for the onslaught of the winter that was just beginning.

Waggit awoke one morning, stretched, yawned, and sniffed the air. It was very cold and damp and had a strange smell to it. As was often the case, he was the first one of the team to wake up, apart from the Lady

Magica, whose turn it was to be on eyes-and-ears duty.

Waggit got up and went to the mouth of the tunnel. He stopped dead in his tracks and gasped. The entry to their home, the bushes that surrounded it, and the trees that were near it were all covered in white. In fact as far as he could see the entire park was the same. It was as if somebody had sucked all the color out of the landscape, and yet it was incredibly beautiful. He ventured out and was amazed to find that the whiteness was deep enough to almost cover his paws. It was also very wet and cold. He struggled up the path at the side of the tunnel to go and see Magica, but his feet kept on slipping and he had to dig his claws into the ground to stop himself from sliding backward. When he finally got to the top he saw her framed by the branches all outlined in white. She looked very beautiful, with a dab of the stuff on her nose. He crawled next to her, bringing down lumps of white as he pushed the branches to get through.

"What happened?" he inquired.

"Nothing much," she said. "It was a pretty quiet night."

"No, I meant where did all this white stuff come

from?" he asked excitedly.

"From the sky, where it always comes from," she replied, somewhat confused by the question. Then it dawned on her. "My dear, you've never seen the Cold White before, have you?"

"Is that what it's called?"

"It's what we call it," she said. "It comes during the Long Cold, but this won't last more than a couple of days. It's too early for it to stay."

"But it's so beautiful," protested Waggit. "I want it to stay."

"Don't worry, my little one," Magica said with amusement. "There will be plenty more before the warm days return. In fact, soon you will wish it would go away."

Waggit thought that this was unlikely and said so. He stood panting with his tongue hanging out, and every time a white flake hit it he felt a tingle. Suddenly Cal and Raz came hurtling out of the tunnel yelling, "The Cold White, the Cold White!" They careened around the clearing in front of the entrance, rolling over and over, laughing with excitement. Waggit ran gleefully to join them. As he got close, Raz stopped and started to dig up the snow ferociously with his front paws. This caused it to shoot out between his back legs, hit Waggit right in the face, and make him sneeze.

"Got you! Got you!" Raz cried triumphantly.

They made so much noise that the other dogs came out, although some, like Gruff, remained at the mouth of the tunnel.

"That's right, go ahead," he grumbled. "Break your legs and expect the rest of us to feed and look after you. That's the sort of responsible behavior we expect from you youngsters!"

"Oh Gruff," Magica said in her most soothing voice, "they're just having fun."

Lowdown and Alicia stood next to each other, looking at the newly whitened landscape. It was always comical to see them together; she long, thin, and haughty, and he short, stocky, and with a mischievous twinkle in his eye.

"D'you know," she shrieked, "that my ancestors came from a land where there was lots of Cold White all the time?" She looked imperiously down on the smaller dog. "Of course I don't suppose you know where your ancestors came from, do you? That's if you had any."

"Well, if I did, I bet they came from a place where the Cold White never got deeper than paw depth." Lowdown chuckled. "If it keeps on coming down like this you're going to have to give me a ride on your back."

"Yeah. In your dreams," was her ungracious reply.

Gordo had now lumbered up to Waggit, Raz, and Cal. There was a bank beside a nearby path, and he flopped down against it. When he got up he left a dog-shaped imprint in the snow. He turned to the others, proud of his trick, but because the snow was thick and wet it had stuck to him in a white coating.

"Hey," said Raz, "you look like you on one side and Waggit on the other."

"Actually," corrected Cal, "you look like you on one side and about five Waggits on the other!"

"You can't have too much of a good thing." Gordo grinned.

"You always did make a good impression, Gordo," said Tazar who had also joined the cavorting dogs, "but don't forget, you guys, that although the Cold White is fun, it also leaves a trail wherever you go that even an Upright could follow. And *will* follow if I'm not mistaken. I don't think that those traps that nearly got

Cal are the last we're going to see of them trying to clear the park of dogs. They do it every year when the leaves come off the trees. They think they can see us better then. Fortunately they smell so bad and make so much noise crashing through the woods that they give us plenty of warning. Even they can follow tracks in the Cold White."

This certainly caused the dogs to pause and look around. Tazar was right as usual. The ground was covered in paw marks. Fortunately it was still snowing heavily, and as they watched the tracks started to fill in.

It snowed for the rest of the day, and Lowdown's prediction came true: it was so deep that it came halfway up his shoulders, making fast movement even more difficult for him than usual. Then as the night settled in, the snow suddenly stopped, the sky cleared, and a full moon shone. Everything was bathed in a blue light that was so bright the trees and benches cast shadows. The branches appeared to have been drawn by somebody using a big stick of chalk. It made the dogs tingle with excitement just to look at it.

"Let's go and see if the water's hard yet," suggested Cal.

"Great idea," said Raz, "Let's go to the Deepwater.

You coming, Waggit?"

"Sure, but why would the water be hard?" Waggit asked.

"It always gets hard when it's cold. Didn't you know that?" chimed in Raz.

He looked at the younger dog's puzzled expression.

"No, I guess you didn't," he said. "This is all new to you, isn't it? Come on, we'll show you."

So off they all trooped in a single line. Cal led, followed by Raz, Waggit, Magica, and even Alicia, who had decided that this would be one of the rare occasions when she joined in. Gordo brought up the rear, mostly because his paws were so huge that they obliterated any tracks made by those in front of him. No one would know, looking at his prints, that more than one dog had passed that way.

Tazar had gone off on one of his mysterious missions. Lowdown had decided to stay in the tunnel because he said he valued breathing too much to risk walking through snow that might be over his head. The thought of spending an evening alone with Gruff, however, was not one that filled him with joy. It was yet another in the many disadvantages of being, as he described it, "economically designed."

When they arrived at the part of the Deepwater where they swam in the summer, Waggit was astounded. It was covered in snow. How could water be covered in anything? Whatever you put on its surface sank, and yet the snow stayed on the top. Then he watched as Raz went up to where the water's edge would be, and with his front right paw scraped away the snow to reveal—hard water! Instead of being liquid it was now milky and solid! Raz took a stone in his mouth, dropped it on the ice, and a pinging sound could be heard echoing across the lake.

"It seems strong enough," he said, and walked out about twenty feet. Waggit couldn't believe his eyes. There was Raz standing where he should be swimming.

"I know!" said Cal, as if struck by a sudden, brilliant idea. "Let's play the sliding game."

"Of course we're going to play the sliding game," said Raz, with a condescending tone. "That's why we're here."

"Okay, Mr. Smarty Hairy Pants. You start," challenged Cal.

"I will if you're too scared to." And Raz made his way up a hill that ran to the water's edge. When he got to the top he turned to face the lake and then ran as fast as he could. By the time he got to the edge of the Deepwater he was going so fast that he couldn't possibly have stopped, and he had no intention of doing so. Instead with a yell of excitement he leapt onto the ice and slid on all fours far out into the Deepwater. He struggled back to the shore, his feet slipping and sliding.

"Okay. Beat that!" he said to Cal.

"No problem whatsoever," the other dog confidently replied, and he also ran up the hill. Cal's descent was even faster than Raz's. He hit the lake's edge at a tremendous speed and shot across the ice, but he was unbalanced.

"*Whoaooooh,*" was all he could say as he lost his footing and tumbled head over tail in a cloud of white.

"I win. I win," cried Raz triumphantly.

"Ow, ow ow," was Cal's pained response.

"Not so fast, brother, you haven't won yet. There's other dogs here waiting for a turn." Lady Magica was already climbing up the hill as she said this. She bounded down the hill in long, graceful steps, quite unlike the uncontrolled gallop of both Cal and Raz. When she hit the ice she glided faster and farther, even doing two 360-degree turns as she flew across the lake's surface, until she slid to a halt many feet farther out than Raz had been.

"Okay, boys, anyone think they can do better than that?" she asked.

"I betcha I can. I betcha anything you like!" said Gordo, full of excited confidence.

He lumbered off at a fairly slow pace, but gravity started to take over, and by the time he was at the bottom it seemed to the spectators as if his legs were trying to keep up with his body. He leapt into the air with a cry of "Yipeeeeeee," hit the ice with a crash, and completely disappeared beneath its surface, sending up a plume of freezing water that soaked the spectators.

"Oh Great Vinda," cried Magica fearfully. "Are you all right? Somebody go get him before he drowns."

But as she said it Gordo rose from the water, pieces of broken ice bobbing all around him, water dripping from his shiny coat. The part of the lake where he'd gone through the ice was not very deep, and he could stand up in it quite easily.

"Oooooh m-m-m-m-my, it's s-s-so c-c-cold!" he said through chattering teeth.

"Well whatd'ya expect," said Alicia, "if you play stupid games like that? You ain't no puppy anymore. You should start acting your age!"

Gordo stepped ashore and shook himself furiously, which only added to Alicia's annoyance, because he was standing directly in front of her. Whether this was deliberate or dumb was always hard to tell with Gordo.

With the ice broken the game ended, and the dogs decided to return to the tunnel. On the homeward journey all attempts at covering up tracks were abandoned as the group joyfully ran through the woods, bringing down great clumps of snow from bushes and branches as they went. They all tumbled into the tunnel, laughing and jostling, energized by the cold, the snow, and the companionship. Even Alicia had lightened up somewhat.

They were not prepared, therefore, for the sight of Lowdown, Gruff, and Tazar, all looking stern and serious.

"I hope you all had fun," Tazar said in his gloomiest voice.

They all nodded.

"Good," the leader continued, "because it may be the last you'll have for a while. As I suspected, the

Ruzelas are having a sweep of the park to clear it of dogs that aren't with Uprights. I was talking to some of the loners today up at the Deepwoods End, and they say that there's been a lot of action up there. Apparently an Upright went to kick a loner, and the dog bit his ankle—purely in self-defense, you understand. But of course nobody believes that Uprights are in the wrong, so it had to be the dog's fault. We've been through this before, and it's not pleasant, I can tell you."

A murmur of concern went through the team.

"What can we do, Tazar?" asked Cal.

"What we can do, my brother, is to do as little as possible. From now on we all stay home. Only designated food parties will go out, and they'll stay in the safest areas, avoiding all paths wherever possible. We take no risks and keep a low a profile. Next thing: while the Cold White is on the ground, anyone who goes outside, either with a food party or for any other reason, makes sure they brush away the tracks they made near the entrance. Use twigs or a branch that still has leaves on it if you can find one. Paw marks anywhere in the vicinity are like saying to the Ruzelas,

'Welcome; come on in.' First thing in the morning, early, Cal, Raz, Waggit, and I will get some more branches to put around the entrance. I want it to be so tight that if a Ruzela tripped and fell against it he wouldn't know that dogs lived here."

Which, as it turned out, was what nearly happened.

8

Battle Plan

The following morning the work party began covering the entrance to the tunnel with as many branches as they could find. The biggest problem was how to hide the opening while at the same time making it possible for the dogs themselves to come and go. In the end Tazar decided that the dogs would use the back entrance, which was much more difficult because it was on a slope that was too steep to climb. But with some well-placed boxes to act as steps it was workable for all the dogs except Lowdown. For him they created a hole in the camouflage large enough to get through but small enough not to be noticed.

When they had concealed the entrance to Tazar's satisfaction each dog took a branch in his or her mouth, and they erased all evidence of their presence by walking backward, moving their heads from side to side, raking the snow. Waggit had the honor of making the final touches. He had found a branch that must have come down before the fall, because it still had its leaves, even though now they were dry and brown. When this was used it gave a much softer and more natural appearance to the raked snow.

Everything was now in place, and all they had to do was sit and wait it out until the rangers finished their sweep. The older members of the team knew from past experience that these operations usually only lasted a couple of days, and as it turned out they didn't even have to wait that long. Later the same afternoon, when they were all in the tunnel either snoozing or washing themselves, Tazar suddenly sat up, his nostrils quivering.

"D'you smell that?" he asked of no one in particular.

All the other dogs lifted their noses.

"Sure do, boss," said Cal. "Uprights, and not too far off."

Then they heard the sound of twigs being snapped and the crunch of snow and ice beneath big work boots. The rangers thought that they were moving through the woods in complete silence, but to the sensitive ears of the dogs they sounded like the Macy's Thanksgiving Day Parade.

"Don't move, stay still, don't pant, and pray to Vinda," Tazar whispered.

They lay there quietly, none of them so much as twitching a muscle, as the noise got louder and louder. Suddenly there was a yell, a huge crash, and a large boot, along with the leg to which it was attached, smashed through the twig covering and into the tunnel.

"Ouch," cried the owner of the leg. "Ouch, ouch. Help me! I slid down the bank and I think I've twisted my ankle."

Although the dogs didn't understand any of this, not being able to speak human language, it was pretty obvious to them what had happened. During the day the sun must have melted the surface of the snow, which had frozen again as the afternoon cooled and formed a treacherous icy surface on the slope above the tunnel's entrance. A ranger had slipped on this and now lay injured, unable to get up. The team heard two of his colleagues clambering down to help their fallen comrade.

"Are you okay, Dick?" one of them said.

"Do I look okay?" he replied crossly. "One ankle's swelling up, and the other's stuck in these stupid bushes."

"What's down there?" asked the other helper.

"Never mind what's down here," said the injured man. "It's just one of those disused tunnels that we were going to clean out before the budget cuts. Come on, help me get up."

As the two rangers helped the third one to his feet he pulled his trapped boot out of the branches. The dogs held their breath, knowing that this could bring all the camouflage crashing down, but both their luck and the structure held. The rangers left, the injured one hopping on one leg with his arms around the shoulders of his workmates. When they could no longer be heard or smelled, the dogs sighed in relief.

"Whew, that was a close one," said Lowdown.

"I was scared," said Magica.

"I'd've protected you. I wouldn't have let them take you," Gordo gallantly claimed.

"The good news," said Tazar, "is that most likely they won't come back here. They'll think they've already checked this area. We can probably move around a bit more freely now, but we should be careful all the same."

Tazar decided that Cal, Raz, and Magica should go out hunting and foraging, while he and Waggit repaired the hole in the entrance made by the ranger's foot. Although he was fairly certain that the immediate danger of capture was over, Tazar was always cautious, and he did not want a hole in the protective covering as big as a size-twelve boot to stay there for long. It was fixed in no time, and then the leader went off on another mystery journey. Since Waggit had no other duties for the day he settled down in the warmth and safety of the tunnel next to Lowdown.

"If they had found us, what would've happened?" he asked.

"Well, I doubt they would've gotten the whole team, but probably most of us. They have these net things they throw over you, and you get all tangled up in them so you can't move," the older dog replied.

"Who do you think would've escaped?" Waggit asked.

Lowdown thought for a moment.

"Cal and Raz might've gotten away out of the back entrance, although if the Ruzelas were smart they'd've had someone waiting there. But those two are fast and they might've made it. Magica too maybe."

"I'm fast," protested Waggit.

"Yes you are," said Lowdown, "but you're also scared, and that would have stopped you long enough for them to get you."

Waggit was about to deny this when he realized that, upsetting though it might be, Lowdown was right. He would have been paralyzed by fear if the men had come into the tunnel.

"Now, Tazar," Lowdown continued, "Tazar would've chosen to fight. He hates them so much he would've tried to take just one with him, even though he knows he couldn't. They'd've got him with one of those stinger things they have that make you go to sleep, and that would've been that."

Waggit looked over at Gordo, who was on his back, legs in the air, snoring peacefully.

"They wouldn't have needed stingers for Gordo," he said to Lowdown, and they both giggled.

"Yeah, no way he would've escaped, although they might've let him go because he was too heavy for them to carry to the cages," said Lowdown.

"They put you in cages? Like the one that Cal got stuck in?" asked Waggit. Lowdown nodded.

"What do they do next?" Part of Waggit wanted to know, but another part was scared to hear the answer.

"They load them on to one of their big rollers and take you to the Great Unknown."

"Where is that and what happens there?" Waggit couldn't stop himself now.

"Nobody knows," said Lowdown patiently. "That's why it's called the Great Unknown. Nobody who goes inside ever comes back. All we know about it comes from one of the loners that they captured. As they was unloading him off the roller they dropped his cage, the door flew open, and he was away. It took him two days to get back here, what with avoiding Uprights and getting lost and so on. Anyway, he said it was a big, dark, scary building, but as to what goes on inside it I leave to your imagination."

Waggit shuddered, for the imagination of a young

dog is powerful. He lay there nervously panting for a while. Then something else occurred to him.

"Lowdown, why are there loners?" he asked.

"Oh, there's lots of different reasons," Lowdown replied. "Some dogs just don't like other dogs and are always getting into fights with them, so it's best if they stay by themselves. Others think it's safer to be alone; you may not get the support of a team, but you don't get the responsibilities either. You just look out for number one, and that's appealing to this kind of dog. Of course there's others that no team will take, so they don't have a choice."

"Why won't they take them?"

"Waggit, enough already. I'll introduce you to some of them and the answer will be clear, I promise you. Now no more questions!"

There was silence for a while. Waggit shifted around as if trying to get comfortable. Then he said, "Lowdown?"

"Yes, little one?" the older dog said tolerantly.

"Thank you."

"You're welcome."

The repair work that Tazar and Waggit had completed that afternoon didn't last long. The peace of the tunnel was shattered by a crash that took out most of the protective covering as the returning hunters tumbled in, breathless and upset.

"What happened out there?" Lowdown asked, but all three dogs were panting too hard to answer.

Finally Magica managed to say, "Tashi's team. Ambush."

As the dogs regained their breath they told how they had been going toward the Goldenside, well away from Tashi's realm, when they were attacked by Tashi, Tommy Teeth, Spotty the Executioner, and two other toughs called Rashtoon and Medorin. The Tazarians ran, because they were outnumbered, and avoided a major confrontation through Magica's alertness. She had spotted the opposing dogs before they were in fighting range and warned Raz and Cal to run. Because of this the only injuries the dogs sustained were shortage of breath and sore paws.

"This can't go on," said Lowdown angrily.

"And neither will it." The booming voice of Tazar sounded behind them.

They all turned to see the leader, ears pricked, hackles up, and tail high. He was an electrifying sight, clearly angry that his family had been in danger.

"Did you hear what happened, boss?" inquired Lowdown.

"No, I saw. I was on Outlook Rock when it happened. You did well to retreat," he said to the three hunters. "There is no dishonor in avoiding a fight you will lose. Only tussle on your terms and at the time of your choosing. You were not in Tashi's realm, but clearly in Unclaimed Territory. This was an act of provocation that must be answered, and it will be, but on my terms and when I please. Fear not. We will decide this soon, and we will decide it forever."

Not for the first time, Waggit marveled at how Tazar could know everything, be everywhere, and return at exactly the right moment to restore confidence. It was almost magical.

The rest of the evening was spent repairing the damage to the camouflage over the entrance, although nobody did it with much enthusiasm, because the danger from the rangers now seemed less threatening than the menace of the Tashinis. Tazar had insisted on being eyes and ears that night, his mind working over plan after plan for retribution as he kept watch. When morning came it was clear that he had decided upon a strategy.

"This is how we will settle the matter," he announced. Nobody asked which matter he was referring to, for they had all thought of nothing else since the three dogs returned. Well, maybe Gordo had thought about food, and Alicia had thought about how beautiful she was, but the rest of them had focused only on the upcoming battle.

"Our problem," continued Tazar, "is that we are outnumbered and outmuscled. We will be dealing with some of the toughest dogs in the park. That's the downside. The upside is that they are also some of the dumbest. The only ones with anything even approaching smarts are Tashi himself, and Wilbur, who has a sort of cunning that should not be underestimated. Still, Tashi is the brains of the outfit, and if you take Tashi out the others won't know what to do. Oh, they'll bluster and bully, but in the end they'll start fighting one another, because the only thing that keeps them together now is fear of Tashi. Without him they're just a bunch of loners; ignorant loners at that."

The other dogs nodded.

"So this is what we will do," the leader continued. "Tonight all of us, with the exception of Alicia, who will stay here and guard the tunnel, will go over to

Tashi's camp. When we get close Cal, Raz, and Waggit will circle around and climb the large rock where Tashi puts whoever is on eyes-and-ears duty. We have to take out that dog so that he doesn't warn the others. Because you will have a three-to-one advantage, it shouldn't be too difficult, but it needs to be done as quietly as possible. When you've done it one of you will come to the edge of the rock and give us the all-clear."

"Will we have to kill him?" asked Waggit, more casually than he felt.

"You will have to do whatever it takes to stop him from giving a warning," said Tazar calmly. "When the lookout is disabled, Gordo and Magica will drag two of the large trash cans that are on the path near Tashi's camp halfway up the hill, one on either side. It worked before, and it can work again. Lowdown will position himself on the hill opposite the camp, where he can see all the action."

"That leaves you by yourself, boss," said Lowdown.

"That's exactly what I intend. The only way we can win this is if Tashi and I fight to the death, and my plan is to insult him into taking up the challenge. It shouldn't be difficult, because he isn't smart enough to let an insult drop. If the whole team comes out, Gordo and Magica will roll the trash cans down the hill, and we're all going to have to join in the fight. Hopefully the rolling cans and the surprise will cause enough chaos and damage to give us an advantage in a full battle, but I don't think it will come to that. Tashi's too conceited to let a challenge to his honor be answered with help from anyone, even his own team."

There was a silence as the dogs began to realize the significance of Tazar's plan. Magica said in a quiet, serious voice, "Tazar, what happens if . . ."

"If I lose?" said Tazar. "I don't expect to. I'm as big and strong as Tashi, and a whole lot smarter, but you can never tell how these things will go. There's always the possibility of a slip or a wrong move, and if that happens, and he kills me, the rest of you run and meet up with Lowdown. He may be short and old, but he's sharper than all of Tashi's team put together, and if you do exactly what he says he'll save your hides. Of this I have no doubt."

The little dog seemed to visibly grow with this compliment.

"But let's not think of defeat," Tazar said. "The dogs who win are the ones who never think of losing. By tomorrow most of our troubles will be over, and we will live with less fear than today. Let us rest now and prepare our minds for tonight."

"What about food?" said Gordo. "I just thought I should mention it."

"No food today," said Tazar. "You fight better on empty stomachs. Tomorrow we shall feast, I promise you."

"Oh," said Gordo. "Oh well, you're probably right." But you could tell that he was unconvinced.

9

The Mystery
of the Missing Enemy

As night fell the dogs gathered themselves together in the tunnel. You could feel the tension as each animal thought about his or her role in the upcoming action. Dense clouds raced across the sky, causing the moon to go in and out, plunging the landscape into moments of deep darkness. The cold air made the dogs' breath steamlike, and their hurried panting betrayed their nervousness. They were eager to leave and yet unwilling to go to what could easily become a disaster.

"Okay now," said Tazar, "we all know what we have

to do. Stick to the plan as far as possible, but be prepared for the unexpected. Good luck to us all. In a few hours we will be leading a safer and freer life, and that's worth whatever sacrifice the evening demands."

They moved out in silence. At that hour of the night and time of year there were hardly any people around, and so they were safely able to make swift use of open ground. Tashi's team lived in what looked like a large clump of bushes at the bottom of a hollow in the ground. If you inspected the shrubs more closely, however, you would see that at the back of the thicket, where the undergrowth grew against a rock face, there was a passageway that led to a cave formed out of the vegetation. It was neither as secure nor as cozy as the Tazarians' tunnel, since both wind and rain could pass through, especially in the winter, when there were no leaves to protect it. Its chief advantage was its nearness to the park restaurant that was the team's chief source of food.

Because it was in a bowl the camp was also easy to defend. The top of the rock that enclosed one end was where the Tashinis placed their sentry, and the only access to this position was up the slopes on either side that formed the walls of the hollow. This was the route that Cal, Raz, and Waggit had to take in order to neutralize the sentry on duty that night.

Once everyone else was in position the three dogs silently made their way up, crawling on their stomachs, using whatever cover there was, and moving rapidly during the periods of darkness when the moon disappeared behind clouds. Inch by inch, foot by foot, they gradually ascended. They finally made it to where they had a clear view of the watchdog in his position, or would have if there had been one. The top of the rock was empty.

"What do we do now?" whispered Raz.

"Waggit, go quietly down and tell Tazar that there's no eyes and ears here tonight," said Cal.

"Okay," said Waggit, relieved that the possibility of a fight had been postponed. On his way down he passed Gordo, who was carefully and quietly pushing a large trash can into position. When Waggit got to Tazar and informed him of the situation, the leader looked puzzled.

"Tashi may be careless about some things," he whispered to the younger dog, "but not about security. This is very strange."

Suddenly from the side of the bowl that Waggit had

just run down came a cry of "Ooooohhhhhhh!!!!" and a crashing and clanging as both Gordo and his trash can tumbled down the hill.

"Oh-oh, that's blown it," said Tazar, no longer bothering to whisper. "Get ready, everyone!"

Waggit stood paralyzed with fear, his eyes wide open, because he realized he was standing next to the first target that the Tashinis would attack: his leader, Tazar. He waited for the enemy to come running out of their camp, but none did. Everyone stood for a moment in complete silence.

"Tashi, you coward," yelled Tazar, "show us you're not the miserable scurry the whole park thinks you are. Come out and fight like a dog!"

Everyone waited, tensed and ready to fight, but there was no response.

"If you don't show yourself now, my team will take over the feeder. It will be ours," challenged Tazar, but there was still no response.

By now Lowdown had left his position on the adjoining hill and was standing by Tazar's side.

"It could be a trap, boss," he said. "Why don't you let me go and take a look? I've got the best chance of getting close without being seen."

"No, Lowdown," said Tazar. "It's too dangerous, and you're not quick enough to make an escape if you have to."

"If I have to make an escape, then at least we've flushed them out, and I'll rely on you all to rescue me," he replied.

"Hmm," said Tazar. "I suppose you've got a point. Okay then, but be careful."

"It's my second name," chuckled Lowdown as he started out toward the bushes.

Even for a dog as small and close to the ground as Lowdown, there was not much cover to help him to approach the camp undetected, but the little dog did the best he could. Everyone held their breath until he got to the bushes. Then he disappeared. A couple of minutes later, there was a cry from the center of the thicket.

"It's empty," came Lowdown's voice. "There's no one here." There was a pause. "And it's disgusting!"

The rest of the dogs ran into the bushes, eager to see the enemy's camp. It was, as Lowdown said, pretty awful. Tazar was a stickler for keeping the tunnel clean and neat, but this clearly was not a concern of the Tashinis, for the place was scattered with bones and bits of partially eaten food, along with old pizza boxes and other containers, as well as items of old human clothing, including a shoe.

"Where could they all be?" wondered Cal.

"You don't think," offered Magica hesitantly, "that they could be doing exactly what we're doing and that they're at our place right now?"

"Dear Vinda, you may be right," said Tazar in alarm.

"Alicia!" gasped Raz.

"Let's go," snapped Tazar, and the team started as one to run back to the Risingside, heedless of the dangers of passing cars or Uprights. As they rounded the bend that led to the tunnel they pulled up short at the sight of Lady Alicia lying in front of the entrance, licking her paws without a care in the world. She looked up.

"Didja get 'im?" she casually inquired. "Is he dead?"

"Not only did we not get him," said Tazar, "we didn't even find him. No one was home."

"Well, where else could they be?" asked Alicia. "They'd never leave that place without someone to look after it."

"That's true," said Tazar. "Even if they had been intent on raiding our place, they would have left someone on guard back there. Let's think what this could mean."

The dogs fell silent as each one grappled with this strange situation. It was a mystery, and mysteries were always unnerving.

"I don't think well on an empty stomach," said Gordo. Bits of garbage were still sticking to his coat where he had collided with the trash container.

"You don't think well on any kind of stomach," said Cal, accurately if somewhat unkindly.

"I think worse on an empty one," insisted Gordo.

"Let's sleep on it," said Tazar, "but tonight I want two on eyes and ears. Cal and Raz, you take it and stay alert. This could be some kind of trick."

When dawn broke a few hours later most of them were still sleeping. Cal and Raz, who had spent a tiring night on duty, came down to the tunnel exhausted.

"Waggit, take over, will you?" pleaded Cal.

"Sure thing," Waggit said, and scrambled up the slope. He liked sentry duty, especially during the daylight hours. He felt safe in the undergrowth on top of the tunnel, and it was interesting to see the life of the park unfolding before his eyes.

Waggit scanned the view from side to side as he had

been taught, noting anything unusual. Suddenly, out of the corner of his eye, he thought he could see a shape moving, dark against the whiteness of the snow. He looked again. Yes, there was definitely something there—some kind of animal moving in the woods close to the tunnel. He didn't want to use the alarm system because the tumbling cans would alert whatever was out there as well as the sleeping dogs below, so he crept very quietly down to the interior. His white coat made him almost invisible against the snow, and the intruder clearly didn't notice his movements.

As he reached Tazar's sleeping form, the black dog opened one eye.

"What is it?" he said.

"There's something out there. I'm not sure what, but some kind of animal, and it's checking out the tunnel," said Waggit.

"Okay, let me take a look," said Tazar. He climbed up the slope and then stopped, his head tilted to one side inquisitively, but without fear. When Waggit scrambled to his side he saw that a nervous brown female dog was facing him, ears down, quivering and crouching close to the ground. Her whole body language was submissive, and as she crept forward the snow piled up in front of her chest.

"A good morning to you, sister. Why the pleasure of your company so early this day?" asked Tazar.

The brown dog looked up at him with frightened eyes. She went to speak, but no sound came out.

"Don't be frightened, sister. We're not going to eat you," said Tazar in his most reassuring voice.

"Please, sir," she finally whispered, "I want to join your team."

"I've seen you before," said Tazar. "You're one of the loners that lives on the Goldenside, near the Deepwoods End."

"I used to," she said, "but I can't live there no more. That's why I need to join you."

"Something bad must have happened if a loner wants to be part of a team," said Tazar.

"Very bad, sir," agreed the female. "Very bad indeed. It's the Ruzelas; they hit the Goldenside hard. They got many loners and took all of Tashi's team. They got them with those big nets as they tried to escape. I saw them being loaded into a roller. It was horrible to see, sir."

"You say they got *all* of Tashi's team?" asked Tazar incredulously.

"All the ones I know," the female replied.

"Well, that would explain a lot," said Tazar. "But you are welcome. Come, come with us, and meet your new brothers and sisters."

Tazar, Waggit, and the female entered the tunnel. The rest of the team looked curiously at the stranger, who was so uncomfortable that she seemed to be praying for a hole in the earth to appear and swallow her up.

"Dogs, listen up," said Tazar commandingly. "This is a sister who has asked if she can join our group. She has lived in the park for many risings as a loner, but now she wishes to be a team member, even though it's against her nature. She realizes now that the power of the team is the only way to survive the threat of the Ruzelas. Tell me, sister," the leader continued, "what's your name? How shall we call you?"

The female muttered something beneath her breath.

"Speak louder. You are among friends, among your family," said Tazar.

"Please, sir, I have no name. Loners don't need names."

"Well, we must give you one," said Tazar, "for you are alone no longer."

"Once a loner, always a loner," said Gordo in a surprisingly philosophical frame of mind.

"Gordo, my friend," cried Tazar with delight, "you have become mighty skilled in the naming of names."

"I have?" said Gordo with surprise.

"Indeed you have. You gave us Waggit's name, and now you've named our sister here."

"I did?" Gordo was now completely mystified.

"I thought I heard you say she would always be Alona, and so she shall be. May I present to you the Lady Alona," said Tazar with a flourish.

There was a chorus of yips and howls, and cries of "Lady Alona," and "Good name," and "Welcome to the family." The reception was so warm, it was impossible for even a dog as shy as Alona not to relax a little and begin to feel safe. Even Alicia, seeing no competition in the plain, shy little thing, was hospitable in a condescending sort of way.

Meanwhile Gordo was sitting with a frown on his face, scratching his ear in confusion, and still trying to work out his part in the naming ceremony.

"Lowdown . . ." he said as the short dog walked by.

"Don't worry about it," Lowdown said without stopping.

"One more thing." Tazar interrupted the celebrations. "Our new sister told me something that I should pass on to you. While on the Goldenside, on her last day as a loner, she saw something that, if it's true, is of interest to us all."

"It is true." Alona spoke more firmly than at any time since her arrival. "I only speak the truth. I saw it, sir," she insisted. "I saw it as clear as I see you now."

"What?" said Lowdown. "What did she see? What did you see?"

"What she saw," said Tazar, "was all of Tashi's team being captured by the Ruzelas and taken away in rollers. *All* of them, she says."

"Including Tashi himself?" asked Cal.

"That I don't know," admitted Alona. "I didn't actually see them put him in the rollers, but there was no one left. They must've got him."

"Whad'ya think, boss?" said Lowdown.

"Well," said Tazar, "it would explain why the camp was empty when we got there, but on the other hand, it hasn't been my experience that problems solve themselves as easily as that, so I'll just let this sit for a while."

"My feelings exactly," agreed Lowdown. "If it seems

to be too good to be true it probably ain't. Not, of course," he added hurriedly, "that there's anything good about dogs being captured by the Ruzelas, even Tashi's gang of delinquents."

Tazar and Lowdown walked away from the main group. Waggit had noticed how much the leader depended upon the wisdom of the smaller dog in times of uncertainty, and not knowing where the enemy was or what he was doing made Tazar anxious.

"So you don't think she's telling the truth?" he asked Lowdown.

"I dunno, boss. Like you said, if it *is* true it could explain a lot, but I would hate for us to relax and let our guard down, which may be exactly what Tashi wants us to do. As for Alona, she's a strange one all right, but then, so am I, and if we said 'No strange ones' we'd have to disband the team altogether."

"I tell you one thing," said Tazar. "I don't think she's a spy. She's a genuine loner. I've seen her many times at the Deepwoods End, always by herself, always staying clear of everyone, Uprights and dogs alike."

"Well, if I was you, boss, which I'm glad I ain't," Lowdown continued, "I'd maintain vigilance, but in a low-key kinda way. Double up on eyes and ears at night, have a quiet word with Cal, and maybe even Waggit. We don't want Alona thinking we don't believe her, 'cause she's going to have a hard enough time fitting in as it is."

Both dogs stood quietly outside the tunnel entrance for a moment.

"One other thing, boss." Lowdown broke the silence hesitantly. "It might be a good idea if you spent more time around the camp than you have lately. If we're attacked and you're in some far corner of the park you ain't gonna be much use to us, and, honestly, I'm not sure we could win without you."

"I have things I have to do that you don't know about. You're going to have to trust me on that," said Tazar mysteriously and somewhat defensively.

"I don't doubt it," said Lowdown. "All I'm saying is, we need you."

The rest of the day passed uneventfully, much of it spent trying to get Alona to relax. Lowdown had accurately predicted the difficulty she would have doing this, and with the best will in the world, there was little the other dogs could do to help her fit in to their communal life. She had realized that for her own survival she needed the protection only a group could give her against the two great enemies—the Ruzelas and hunger. Being part of a team even helped combat the cold, something that was becoming a problem for her. But despite all these obvious advantages, she had spent most of her life by herself, depending on no other dog and trusting none either. This was something you couldn't just put down like a stick you were carrying; it would take time for her to make a big adjustment.

Waggit felt sorry for her. He knew from his own experience how hard it was to commit to being part of the team. He tried to make conversation with her.

"I like your name," he said.

There was no reply.

"They gave me a name too," he continued. "I didn't have one either when I came here. Mine's Waggit."

Still nothing.

"I wasn't too sure of it at first." He pressed on despite the one-sided nature of the conversation, "But now I like it. It's sort of masculine. Yours is very feminine."

Waggit had run out of topics, for his social skills were not great. So he just stood there, his tail wagging anxiously.

Suddenly Alona whispered, "Tazar don't believe I saw what I saw."

"You think?" said Waggit, completely taken aback.

"He don't trust me," she continued in a low voice, "and if he don't trust me I can't stay here; I can't be a team member if I'm not trusted. It's all about trust."

Now it was Waggit's turn to fall silent. He sat down and scratched his ear, which always seemed to help the thought process. After careful consideration of her statement he said, "I don't think it's that he doesn't trust you. When it comes to security Tazar's very careful. He'll take risks, but he likes to have all the facts before he does."

"Well, he's going to have to trust me on this one. Nobody's coming back from where those dogs went to tell him I was right."

This ended the conversation, such as it was, and the two wandered apart.

The meal that night was sparse. The hunting party of Cal, Raz, and Magica had returned with an assortment of small animals, none of which provided much meat. Tazar, who had taken Lowdown's advice and stayed around for most of the day, authorized the supplementation of the meager spread with food out of the store. When it was really cold the dogs kept any food left over from previous nights in a hole in the ground that they had dug and covered with branches. It was placed so that the sentry on duty could keep an eye on it, for although the branches would have fooled an Upright, any other dog would be able to smell it out easily. Not that there was usually very much in it, mostly items that the dogs didn't like—stale bread, carrots that had fallen off carriages that the horses pulled, or the occasional half-eaten apple tossed away by a human. It was a rare occasion that the store contained their favorite food—meat in any form.

As they were about to sit and consume their modest meal, a long and lonesome howl shattered the silence of the night. All the dogs rushed to the entrance to see where the forlorn sound came from. Sitting on a rock not far from the tunnel was Tashi, his head pointed to the sky, his lips pursed, and his ears flat to his head. Next to him was his evil lieutenant, Wilbur. When he realized who was there, Tazar stepped forward.

"Tashi, we heard bad times have fallen on your team. Indeed we heard that you yourself had been taken," he said.

"The Ruzela ain't born yet what can take me," replied Tashi belligerently. "But the team, yeah, it's tough, but they've gone."

"It's a tragedy."

"It's a pain in the tail," answered Tashi, "but it ain't a tragedy. You know you've got to be sharp to survive in the park, and those guys were good, but they just weren't sharp enough."

"What Tashi means," added Wilbur in his obsequious voice, "is that though he's personally devastated by the loss of dear friends, he feels you have to move on." Wilbur spent much of his time trying to explain what Tashi meant.

"Yeah, move on," said Tashi. "You got to move on."

"Why didn't they get you two as well?" asked Tazar.

"Well, we was sharp," said Tashi. "We saw them coming. We was up on the big rocks overlooking the fountain, so we lay low until they went."

"You didn't try to warn your team?" Tazar was astonished.

"Listen," barked Tashi, "the first law of survival is:

look after number one. You've got to take . . . what is it you have to take for your own life?" he asked Wilbur.

"Responsibility," the other dog replied.

"Yeah, that's it. Responsibility. It's every dog for himself," Tashi explained, with the air of one well versed in philosophy.

"This is not to mean, of course," continued Wilbur, "that we wouldn't have warned them if it had been at all physically possible, but frankly, it was too dangerous."

"Did the Ruzelas get them all?" asked Tazar.

"It pains me to say that they got every last one," Wilbur replied with very little pain in his voice.

"Look, let's cut out the garbage," said Tashi, with obvious impatience. "What's done is done. There's no use chewing on old bones. What this means is that Wilbur and me don't have any soldiers left to defend the realm, so we was wondering whether you all would be interested in joining our team."

"And what team would that be?" inquired Tazar.

"Me and Wilbur's team of course," replied Tashi, slightly mystified.

"As I understand it your team is in the Great Unknown. We seem to be the only team in this part of the park, and we've already joined us," said Tazar. "So it would be more the case of *you* joining *our* team—if we invited you, of course."

Tashi paused to consider this statement, which obviously put the situation for him in a completely new light.

"Of course," oozed Wilbur, "it would be an honor for us to be a part of your team, but we just felt that with Tashi's unparalleled skills in leadership it would be to your team's advantage to place themselves under his protection. We would, of course, Tazar, offer you a position of the highest rank within the new organization."

"Tashi's not a leader." Tazar growled, getting angry now. "He's a bully. He rules by fear and always has. Anyone who abandons his team to the fate of the Great Unknown in order to save his own flea-bitten hide is no leader in my book."

There were murmurs of agreement from the Tazarians, who had moved behind Tazar. They advanced a step or two closer to Tashi and Wilbur. Both dogs on the rock regarded this as an aggressive movement. Their hackles rose, and Wilbur took a defensive position behind Tashi.

"Now, fellers," he said from behind Tashi's back. "Let's talk this over. I'm sure we can come to a suitable arrangement."

"The only suitable arrangement I'm interested in is for you to get out of our realm right now," said Tazar.

Tashi stood up on the rock and looked down on Tazar, his small, mean eyes blazing and his strong, muscled body taut and ready to spring.

"You always was a fool, Tazar, and weak as well," he growled. "You'll live to regret this. There's dogs who would kill to live in my realm; I'll get another team together in no time, and then we'll see who joins who."

"You don't have a realm," answered Tazar. "The realm you did have is up for the taking by anyone who wants it and can defend it, and there's nothing you can do about it. As of now you're just a couple of loners."

Tashi glared terrifyingly at Tazar, and said through clenched teeth, "You are dead, Tazar. You are dead."

He turned and, closely followed by Wilbur, disappeared into the night.

10

Hidden Treasure

The Tazarians were proud of the way their leader had handled the situation. Tazar himself didn't share their satisfaction. Perhaps it might have been smarter to be less confrontational. He knew that he had humiliated and angered Tashi, and that because of this the other dog would be determined to get revenge.

"I should've treated him different, Lowdown," Tazar said. "I know I hackled him up, but I was so angry at the way he just abandoned his team. He was their leader, and he should've died for them."

"Like you said, boss, Tashi's a bully," replied Lowdown, "and the trouble with bullies is, they don't listen to reason. They only respect power and Tashi's got to realize now that he ain't got none."

"But that'll eat at him too. I was wrong," said Tazar. "Tashi isn't a loner and never will be. He's a general without an army, and he'll never rest until he gets one again."

The two dogs fell silent. It seemed to Lowdown that life in the park was a never-ending series of threats. Sometimes he felt so tired of meeting its daily challenges, and yet he really had no alternative. He was too old and had lived for too long as a team member to become a loner. Besides, he liked the Tazarians. And the only other way out was capture by the authorities and the uncertain future of the Great Unknown. So there was no use being downhearted.

It seemed as if Tazar had read his mind.

"There's no use fretting about it now," he said. "At least we've got Tashi off our backs for the time being. Let's go join the others."

With the capture of Tashi's team the rangers had pretty much abandoned their hunt for strays. It was now possible to move more freely throughout the park without worrying about wandering into Tashi's territory. Even the weather moderated, causing small animals to come out of their holes and be hunted. The greater freedom of movement helped with the food supply in other ways as well. There were certain areas of the park where well-meaning humans came to feed the birds with small piles of bread, nuts, and sometimes pieces of bacon fat. While each pile of food was not great, if the team had access to all of them, it could make a difference. The only problem was that you had to fight off the birds for which they were intended. This wasn't as easy as it sounds, and many a dog's ear had been painfully pecked in the process. Since the bird food was usually too small for the dogs to transport back to the tunnel, Tazar allowed it to be eaten on the spot.

The dogs scavenged in pairs, with Alona, always the odd dog out, joining up with whichever couple invited her. On one such day she was out with Waggit and Lowdown.

She was a strange animal to be sure. She combined extreme shyness with a short temper, and had a habit of defending herself when nobody had attacked her. Despite this, Waggit liked her. She seemed honest, honorable, and was even, on rare occasions, funny. She always walked about three paces behind whomever it was she accompanied, and called everyone "sir," except of course Magica and Alicia, to whom she hardly ever spoke.

On this particular day Waggit and Lowdown had decided to familiarize themselves with the portion of their area that was formerly in Tashi's territory. They were excited about being able to go as they pleased without always having to look over their shoulders. Of course, they still had to be wary of human beings in any form, and the police and park rangers in particular, but the dogs were used to this. They were trotting at a brisk pace down by the lake where the boats had been pulled up for the winter and now looked like sleeping turtles resting one upon another. Suddenly Alona stopped and sniffed the air. Because she was in her normal position behind them Waggit and Lowdown didn't notice right away. Then they both turned to see her nose working furiously.

"What're you picking up, Alona?" asked Lowdown.

There was no reply, just more furious sniffing, her head turning from side to side as she tried to locate the direction of the scent.

"Alona, talk to me," said Lowdown.

"It's around here somewhere, sir," she said.

"What is, Alona?" asked Waggit.

More silence.

Suddenly she moved forward swiftly, past the other two dogs, her head held high as she followed the scent.

"This way," she said. "Follow me."

Waggit and Lowdown did as she said, the two of them now several paces behind her. Then they could smell it as well, and the three of them started to run toward the unmistakable odor of meat.

"It's Stashi's tash," Alona said, panting from the exertion.

"It's what?" asked Lowdown.

"I think she means Tashi's stash," said Waggit helpfully.

"Let's hope," said Lowdown, for Alona showed no interest in correcting herself.

She suddenly stopped. The scent was stronger now, but they couldn't tell exactly where it came from. They were in a lightly wooded area near one of the roads that ran across the park. Getting an accurate fix on the source of the tantalizing meat smell was made more difficult by the light covering of snow that remained on the ground. Not only does snow have an odor all of its own, which humans can't detect but dogs can, it also traps other scents, all of which added to a smelly confusion.

"Yes, I think you're right. We're close, because I saw them bringing it here too," Alona said.

The problem with talking to loners was that they tended to carry on conversations inside their heads that they assumed you could hear. It was unnerving when she answered a question that nobody had asked.

"You saw who bringing what where?" asked Lowdown, getting somewhat irritated.

"Swag, sir," she replied. "Stuff they got from the feeder. Lots of it."

"How did you see them?" asked Waggit.

"You still think I'm a spy, don't you?" She was suddenly angry. "You think that the reason I know where they took it is because I used to be one of them. Go on, admit it; I know what you're thinking."

"Alona," said Waggit patiently, "if I thought you were one of them because you knew where they took it, then you'd know where they took it, which, if you don't mind me reminding you, you don't, which is why we're standing here trying to find where they took it."

Waggit's grammar may have left a lot to be desired, but his logic was solid. "Oh," was all Alona could say.

In the meantime Lowdown had gone off to investigate a hole between the roots of a tree. Suddenly there was a sliding sound, a muffled cry, and Lowdown disappeared from sight. Waggit and Alona ran to the hole and peered in.

"Lowdown-down-down, are-ar-ar you-ou-ou okay-ay-ay?" Waggit's voice echoed as he stuck his head in the hole.

"Okay?" Lowdown's voice boomed back, sounding much bigger than usual. "I'm so okay I could spend the rest of my days in here. Come on in and see what I mean."

It was a much tighter squeeze for Waggit than for Lowdown, but the ice surface that had made Lowdown slide into the hole helped Waggit too. He landed with a thump onto a hard rock floor and looked around.

"Oh my!" was all he could say.

The two dogs were in a natural cave, but it wasn't the cave itself that was remarkable, as much as its contents. There was meat, lots of it, in almost every form. There were sausages of all descriptions, slabs of bacon, packages of hot dogs and hamburgers, even a couple of steaks. For two carnivores it was the equivalent of heaven. The reason that the scent of meat was so strong was also apparent to the dogs. Some of it had either been put in the cave before the temperature dropped enough to preserve it, or it had already been rotten when it was "liberated" from the restaurant's Dumpsters.

Waggit looked around in awe.

"Gordo will pass out with pleasure when he sees this," he said.

"For that to happen we're going to have to make that hole a lot bigger," Lowdown remarked with a snicker.

Alona now stuck her head into the hole.

"Pardon me for bothering, but are you both all right?" she asked. Then, as her eyes accustomed themselves to the darkness she said, "Goodness, I didn't realize they had stashed this much. No wonder they always fought so hard to keep the feeder in their realm."

"There must be enough here to feed everyone in the park for the rest of the Long Cold," Waggit said excitedly.

"I only wish that were true, little one," said Lowdown in his wisest voice, "but it won't even keep our team for long. It looks like a lot, but we have many mouths to feed, and, no, Alona, I'm not blaming you, accusing you, or whatever else that look you just flashed me meant."

Alona's ears went flat on her head with embarrassment.

"No, sir. I'm sorry, sir. I'll be grateful for anything I get," she said.

"Let's face it," said Lowdown, "if it wasn't for you we might not have found the stash in the first place, so in fact *we're* beholden to *you*."

Alona muttered something about it being nothing at all, and that they were welcome, and then her head disappeared.

"Great Vinda, you have to be careful what you say in front of her," said Lowdown. "Talk about touchy!"

"Well, you know, it takes a loner a while to adjust," said Waggit. "They're not used to being around other dogs."

"Oh," said Lowdown, "and when did you become such an expert on loners?"

"It was just something I heard." It was Waggit's turn

to be embarrassed now. "I've been around a while now," he continued defensively.

"Yes, you have," said Lowdown. "In fact you've been around in this cave much too long. We've got to get back to camp to tell the others about our discovery, and then haul it back to the Risingside."

Getting out of the cave was a lot harder than getting in. Waggit tried to stretch up and get a grip on the sides of the hole to pull himself out, but he couldn't get high enough. He and Lowdown pushed a box of frozen hamburgers just below the hole, and this gave him enough of a paw-hold that he could pull himself out. For Lowdown, however, the situation was impossible, and they decided that Waggit and Alona should go back to the tunnel and get help, not just to get the food out of the cave, but Lowdown too.

"You will be okay, won't you?" asked Waggit. "We won't be long."

"Take your time," said Lowdown. "Don't you worry about me. If necessary I'll snack my way out of any emergency!"

"Okay." Waggit chuckled. "But don't eat so much that we can't get you through the hole."

When Waggit and Alona got back to the tunnel the

whole team was there. Gasps of surprise and whoops of joy greeted the news of the discovery, and there was much praise of Alona for finding the hidden treasure. With each compliment she seemed to become more uncomfortable, so everyone concentrated on how to get the meat back to the camp.

Transporting it wasn't a problem; one of the Skurdies had left a broken milk crate near the camp. Gordo volunteered to push it over the ice and snow to the hole and back again. Tazar accepted his offer but wisely said that he thought another dog should go with him for protection. Whether it was for Gordo's protection or the protection of the meat, the leader didn't say, but most of the other dogs had their own ideas.

The biggest problem was getting the food out of the hole and into the crate, and the only solution to this seemed to be putting both Waggit and Magica back down there. They would pass each piece up to Alicia. She had a long and elegant neck that would probably stretch deep enough into the cave to be able to retrieve the items from the mouths of the other two dogs. Alicia wasn't too keen on this, because she thought the chances of getting dirty were pretty high, but she wanted her share of the food, so she reluctantly agreed. How they were going to get Lowdown out was undecided as they all trooped off to the Goldenside. Gruff stayed as a sentry to sullenly guard the tunnel until their return.

The dogs ran ahead to the cave, leaving Gordo behind, puffing and panting as he pushed the milk crate with his nose. The problem was that it kept on sliding off in a different direction from the one that he had intended, so the faster he tried to push it, the slower he went. When they returned to the stash Tazar put his head into the hole. There was a short, muffled conversation with Lowdown that the others couldn't hear, but when their leader pulled his head back out, he was frowning.

"That's quite a find," he said. "In fact it's almost too much of a find. There's no way we can store all of that. We're going to have to leave some of it behind."

Gordo, who had finally puffed his way up, suggested in a panic-stricken voice that he would enlarge their stash in order to take it all.

"No way, Gordo," said Tazar, "the ground's frozen solid. Even your great paws couldn't make any impression on it."

"Well," he replied, "how about we eat all we can

now and then take the rest?"

"So we all end up sick," said Tazar. "That's a great idea!"

"Does that mean no?" asked Gordo.

"That means no," said Tazar firmly.

The dogs set about retrieving as much food out of the cave as they thought would fit into their smaller storage spot near the tunnel. When they had filled the milk crate nearly to the top, Tazar called a halt. However, the problem of reclaiming Lowdown still hadn't been solved. The team was thinking about what to do next when Alona came back with a long, dead vine in her mouth. She dropped it in front of Tazar.

"Would this help, sir?" she asked quietly.

"Help?" exclaimed Tazar. "Help? It's perfection. I never saw a finer solution to a problem in my entire life. The team thanks you profoundly!"

"You're welcome, sir," Alona mumbled. Tazar was now busy organizing the rescue, ordering Cal, Raz, Magica, and Waggit to grab one end of the vine in their mouths, and instructing Lowdown to hold on tight to the end that had been lowered into the hole. Fortunately Lowdown had more than a little terrier in him, and once his jaws were clamped around anything, it was almost impossible to loosen them without his consent.

Once everyone was in position, Tazar gave the dogs the order to pull. They did this somewhat overenthusiastically, and Lowdown popped out of the hole like a cork from a bottle and flew over their heads. He landed heavily on the grass and with a cry of "Ow!" let go of the vine, rolled over a couple of times, got up, shook himself, and sneezed, but was happy to be out.

Tazar ordered everyone to cover the hole with branches and rocks, and then they started back to the tunnel. Gordo pushed the crate with enthusiasm, literally slobbering in anticipation of the evening meal. Cal, Raz, and Magica tried to steer it over the ice and snow, but whether they helped or hindered was debatable. Waggit, Tazar, and Lowdown followed their erratic progress, with Alona bringing up the rear, of course, and at some distance.

When they arrived back at the camp they emptied the contents of the crate into their own stash, which was so small compared to the Tashinis' that nobody would get stuck in it however short his or her legs were. Their haul filled the shallow hole to the top, even after taking out some of the meat for that night's supper. Nobody seemed worried about this, because they all felt they could go back to the cave at any time for more.

Waggit wasn't so sure. It seemed to him that anything in an unguarded hole in the ground in a park full of hungry dogs could never be safe. Even though Alona had helped the Tazarians locate it, the fact of the matter was that it didn't take too long to find it if you had a good nose. And apart from anything else, Tashi and Wilbur knew where it was.

As their stash was being covered up again with branches, Waggit turned to the leader.

"Tazar," he said hesitantly.

"Waggit?" Tazar replied inquisitively.

"We left a lot of food there just now," Waggit said.

"Yes, we did," the leader agreed.

"Well, I was thinking, wouldn't it be better if we moved into Tashi's realm now that it isn't Tashi's realm anymore? That way we could guard the stash, and we'd have the feeder in our own realm when it opened up again." He was nervous at making this suggestion. "It was just a thought."

"It was a very good thought," said Tazar sincerely. He was impressed that Waggit was thinking strategically at such a young age. "There are two things a team needs," he continued. "One is a safe place to sleep, and the other is a good food supply. This place"—he nodded toward the tunnel—"took us a long time to find, and the reason it took a long time was because hardly anybody knew it was here, and that's a good thing. You saw what Tashi's camp was like, and it isn't a coincidence that the Ruzelas got his team and not ours. If you can find a place as secure as this on the Goldenside, then we'll move, but until then we stay put."

"But what about the stash? What about the feeder?" Waggit protested.

"We can always find food somehow," replied Tazar. "We always have, and we probably always will, but to find a camp like this—that's a once-in-a-lifetime find."

Waggit felt strange about this conversation with the dog he admired most in this world, and he couldn't work out why. Then the reason occurred to him—it was the first time he'd found himself disagreeing with Tazar. Little did he know that this was because he was growing up.

11

Two Puppies and a Misadventure

And then the cold came. It was colder than Waggit ever thought it could be. The weather was clear and bright, with blue skies and sunshine, but the temperatures were icy. A constant, biting wind penetrated even the dogs' thick winter coats. It was so cold that they slept in what they called "rotation." Instead of each having their own space in which to stretch out, they huddled together in a circle in the middle of the tunnel. Because the inside of the circle was much warmer, the dogs in the center periodically got up and moved to the outside. This way each dog got a turn at being in the warmest place. The only problem with the system was that you had to climb over the other dogs to get to the outer edge. This was fine if the climber was Magica or Alona, but when either Gruff or Gordo made their way to the outside the other dogs sometimes wondered if the extra warmth was worth the pain.

Even during the day, when they were moving around, it was miserable. There hadn't been any more snow, and what was left from the last storm was now packed down hard and frozen solid. This made going anywhere extremely dangerous, for even long claws could get little grip on the slippery surface. There was always the risk of a broken leg, which is serious enough for dogs who live with people and can get the care of a veterinarian, but for the dogs in the park it could be a death sentence.

The most serious problem was the food shortage. As Lowdown had predicted, the Tazarians' stash was nowhere near enough, and as Waggit had feared, the remaining food in Tashi's stash had been taken, either by Tashi himself or by hungry, scavenging loners. Days went by when each dog had too little to eat or sometimes nothing at all. The colder it got, the more distracted Tazar seemed to be, and the longer his absences became. The team relied on him to organize hunts, using his experience of the park and of the habits of small animals to know where the best spots were likely to be. Adding to all these problems was the fact that there were now two extra, very hungry mouths to feed.

It had happened during the period that the dogs called the Season of Lights. Waggit first noticed it when he and Lowdown were walking along the edge of the Risingside, close to the road that separated the park from the apartment houses. He suddenly became aware of a number of colored lights in the windows, winking on and off. He had also seen similar ones on the collars of the horses that pulled the carriages around the bottom part of the park, and on the carriages themselves. When he asked Lowdown what the lights were for, the older dog said that nobody knew for sure, but there seemed to be a period during the middle of the winter when human beings liked to decorate buildings and other objects with them. He thought it might be because the days were so short at this time, and the darkness so depressing, that it was their way of cheering themselves up. Both dogs agreed that human beings were mysterious creatures who did a lot of unexplainable things.

Several days later Waggit and Lowdown were wandering around on a fruitless scavenge when they came across a large, brightly colored box. At first they thought it might contain food, but then they noticed that it was moving and that strange squeaking sounds were coming from it. Cautiously they approached it, circling around a couple of times before going up to it. As they got closer the movement and sounds stopped. Waggit gripped the top of the container between his teeth and quickly pulled it back to reveal a couple of very young and very frightened puppies.

"What are you two young things doing in here?" asked Lowdown in his softest, kindest voice. The two little creatures huddled closer to each other, making sad little whimpering sounds.

"My oh my," said Lowdown, "I think they may be too young to talk." But later they discovered that this wasn't so; the puppies were just too cold and too frightened to speak.

"What shall we do with them?" asked Waggit. "We can't just leave them here."

"Of course not," agreed Lowdown. "We must take

them back to the tunnel."

"How will we do that? They're too small to walk."

"We'll do what their mother would do under the same circumstances," said Lowdown. "We'll carry them in our mouths, gently though."

He carefully picked up one of the puppies by the loose flesh at the back of its neck. As he did this they both squealed, fearing separation, so Waggit bent tenderly over the other one and lifted it in the same manner. They moved quickly but carefully back to the tunnel, making sure not to slip on the ice and drop their precious packages.

Their arrival got a mixed reception. Alicia haughtily asked what breed the puppies were, while Gruff complained that nowadays they couldn't get enough to feed themselves, without bringing more mouths into the team, particularly those too young to contribute anything to the food supply. Secretly Gordo was thinking the same thing but was too ashamed to admit it, and his initial feeling was changed by Magica's reaction to the puppies, which was one of uncontrolled maternal joy. She cooed, and licked them, and cuddled them in her fur. As Gordo watched her, he too felt a warmth inside that had nothing to do with the weather or anything other than his love for Magica. Tazar was also deeply affected by the two youngsters. The thought of them being left in a box in the bitter winter weather seemed to cause him physical pain.

When they had warmed up and had been given what little food could be spared, the puppies told a tale that was strange to Waggit but all too familiar to the rest of the team. Their earliest memories were of being in a store with lots of other puppies, as well as kittens and birds and a host of other animals. They couldn't remember having a mother, although they were sure they must have had one at some time. One day two humans took them away from the store and brought them to a house where they lived for several days. Then they were put in a box, the same one in which Waggit and Lowdown had found them. They stayed in it for some time, scared and unsure of what was happening.

Suddenly the lid of the box was lifted, and two older humans looked in. The puppies saw that they were in a room, which strangely enough had a tree growing in it that was covered in lights, and there were lots of humans also opening boxes and talking their strange talk that the puppies couldn't understand. After a hectic day of eating and being played with by small humans, the older ones took the puppies in the box to another house, but the following day left them in the park where the two Tazarians found them. They had no idea what had happened and why it had happened to them, but now they felt safe surrounded by their own kind. Soon they fell asleep, nestled in Magica's fur.

Of course nobody questioned that the two puppies would stay and be looked after by the team. Anyone suggesting otherwise would have had to deal with Magica. Unless she was hunting they were always within inches of her. If she felt they weren't getting enough food she would give them hers. In short, she became the mother that they had never known. They were known as Little One and Little Two by the team, and spent their days either playing, and yelping in their squeaky voices, or sleeping for many hours, but always under her protective care.

There was no letup to the bitter weather, and the food problem got worse. It was even difficult to get water. All of the lakes were frozen and the fountains had been shut down at the beginning of the winter. Normally the dogs could take mouthfuls of snow when they were thirsty, but there was none, just hard-packed ice. They survived by chewing on the icicles that had fallen from the ceiling of the tunnel. Everything was frozen: the water was frozen, the food was frozen, the dogs were frozen. It was miserable.

Misery turned to tragedy one day when Magica suddenly had a spasm of pain in her stomach. At first she thought it was because she had eaten very little lately, and that it would go away. But instead it got worse and more frequent, to the point that she could barely stand. She even growled at Little One and Little Two to leave her alone.

Then Gordo came down with the same symptoms. The team was scared. Everyone had heard stories about how whole packs had been wiped out by illnesses that had been passed from one dog to another. Each waited nervously to see who would be next, checking his or her own body for any signs of sickness. Nobody else appeared to be affected, but the two dogs who were seemed to be getting worse by the hour. Magica was unable to stand at all and would go into convulsions. Although not as severe, Gordo's symptoms were the same.

"This is serious," Lowdown whispered to Waggit. "Go see if you can find Tazar."

"Sure thing," said Waggit. "Any idea which way he went?"

"Your guess is as good as mine," answered Lowdown.

As it turned out, Waggit hadn't gone more than a few hundred yards when he came upon Tazar heading toward the tunnel. He quickly explained to the leader what had happened, and they ran back to the camp. Tazar looked at both the stricken dogs and went over to Magica.

"Lady, tell me what you ate since the last rising," he said, but she could only look at him with sad, suffering eyes as her body twitched in pain. He moved to Gordo.

"Gordo, what have you eaten lately?" he asked with a determined but kind manner.

"Just stuff," said Gordo.

"What kind of stuff? I need details," said Tazar.

"Well, let's see . . ." Gordo stopped midsentence as he clenched his teeth with pain.

"Gordo, listen to me," said Tazar. "Did you eat a scurry? You and Magica?"

"We might have," was the reply.

"Might have or did? It's important," continued Tazar.

"Well, yes, we did share one."

"Did you kill it?" asked Tazar.

"Almost."

"Almost!" Tazar was trying to keep his patience with the sick animal. "How in the name of Vinda do you *almost* kill a scurry?"

"Well, it had only just died. It was still warm, so I thought it would be okay," said Gordo.

Tazar had a rule that the team only ate what they had just killed. Only freshly killed meat was likely to be safe, and not bring sickness into the tunnel, whereas something that was already dead could be lethal. Rats were particularly suspect, for there were periods when their bodies were seen around the park in mysteriously large numbers. The dogs didn't know it, but this was the result of park workers putting down poison when the rats got to be a problem.

"Why, Gordo? Why did you do it? You know the rule," said Tazar sorrowfully, his flash of impatience past.

"I was worried about Magica," said Gordo. "She gives nearly all her food to the puppies. I thought she wasn't getting enough to eat, so I went hunting on my own, only I'm not good at it. I'm so clumsy and slow that any animal hears me coming a long way off. Are we going to die, Tazar?"

"Yes, we are," replied Tazar, "but hopefully not for a long while."

Nobody in the tunnel got very much sleep that night. They put both sick dogs in the center of the rotation and kept them there for the entire night, but what with Magica's sudden convulsions and Gordo's groaning there was nothing to do but stay awake and worry.

In the morning things seemed to have improved somewhat. Gordo was actually able to stand a little, and Magica could lick at a piece of ice, although she still lay in pain.

"It's passing through," said Tazar. And then, less certainly, "Please let it pass through."

He sent Alona off with Little One and Little Two so that they wouldn't disturb Magica. The shy, awkward animal seemed to have a connection with the puppies that was difficult for her to make with bigger dogs. The puppies themselves knew that something was wrong, but they weren't quite sure what, and under her watchful eye they played happily beneath some trees just a short distance from the mouth of the tunnel.

Tazar also sent Cal and Raz to scavenge and hunt for food, and the rest of the dogs took turns sitting beside either Magica or Gordo. The worst thing was that there was nothing the dogs could do except to wait and see what happened. Waggit looked down fondly at the big, brown, ungainly dog who was his friend. Gordo lifted his head slightly and looked at him with mournful eyes.

"It was still warm, Waggit," he said. "How could it've been bad?"

"I don't know," Waggit answered. "I would've probably done the same thing myself."

Waggit knew in his heart of hearts that this wasn't true, but he said it to make his friend feel better. It didn't work.

"No you wouldn't," said Gordo. "You're the best hunter on the team. You're fast and quiet, and nothing gets away from you."

"But if there's nothing to hunt, Gordo," Waggit tried again, "it doesn't matter how fast and quiet you are."

"You'd've found something," Gordo insisted. Then he moaned. "It hurts, Waggit, it hurts."

"I know it does," said Waggit. "I wish there was something I could do to take it away from you."

Gordo looked toward the sleeping form of Magica, who lay quite still.

"Well," he said, "at least it seems as if she's not in too much pain now."

"Yes," Waggit agreed, "she looks okay."

"She'll probably be better when she wakes up," said Gordo hopefully.

The day passed uneventfully. Cal and Raz returned empty-mouthed and were promptly sent out again by Tazar, with instructions not to come back until they had some food. Lowdown fussed around the patients, dragging newspaper over them to try to keep them warm. Even Gruff took his turn at comforting Gordo, and Alicia sat motionless, staring at Magica's sleeping form. Tazar and Waggit took turns on sentry duty. It was during one of the times that Waggit was sitting in the tunnel that the puppies returned with Alona. Each had a huge pinecone in his mouth that was almost as big as he was. Little Two dropped his by Magica.

"Mommy Magica, look what Alona found for us," he said excitedly.

Magica did not wake.

"Mommy Magica, wake up," he insisted.

There was still no response from her.

"Please, Mommy Magica, please wake up." The puppy was getting frantic, and his panic alerted the other dogs in the tunnel. He started to lick her face in an attempt to get a response but got nothing.

Then one eye opened, followed by the other. Magica lifted her head slowly and smiled at him.

"Why, little one, what's the matter?" she said in a soft voice.

"I'm Little Two," said the puppy, "and I couldn't get you to wake up."

"Well, you see, I wasn't feeling too good, not quite myself," she said, "but I'm better now."

She got up, shook herself, and licked the puppy back for good measure. A feeling of relief swept through the tunnel. All the other dogs crowded around her, asking if she was really all right, telling her not to tire herself, and offering her pieces of ice for refreshment. All the other dogs, that is, except Gordo, who was still feeling far from well himself, and furthermore was not sure how Magica would treat him, knowing it was his foolishness that had put her through such misery. She spotted him through the crowd that surrounded her and went over to where he lay.

"Gordo," she said affectionately, "get up on those big paws of yours. What're you doing lying there on a beautiful day like today?"

To Gordo it was possibly the most beautiful day of his life. Knowing she had forgiven him brought a lump to his throat.

"I'm still not feeling too good myself," he said when the lump had gone away enough for him to speak.

"Well," said Magica, with a twinkle in her eye, "you must watch what you eat. You never know what you might pick up."

And that was the last thing she ever said on the subject.

It wasn't, however, the last thing that Tazar said. When the others had left the tunnel and he was alone with Gordo, he turned to him with a serious look on his face.

"Don't ever put us through something like that again," he said. "We nearly lost her, you know."

"I never wanted to do her no harm," protested Gordo. "I was just worried she wasn't getting enough to eat."

"We often do the most harm when we least intend it," said Tazar, "but there was something else though, wasn't there? You wanted to be a hero, the great hunter, to look good in front of her."

Gordo hung his head and didn't answer.

"I know how that feels," Tazar continued, "how nice it is to impress, to feel good about yourself. But you have to be true to yourself as well, and you weren't. You're not a hunter, and you know it. You're too big and too slow, and there's nothing wrong with that; it's just the way you were made. Some are born hunters and some are not, and you, my friend, are definitely one of the nots. Magica doesn't love you because you're a hunter; she's a better hunter than you anyway. She loves you because you're you." He paused. "As do we all, you big lug."

"I know it, Tazar," said Gordo dejectedly. "I know all that you just said."

"See, the reason I can say this to you," the leader went on, "is that I'm not much of a hunter myself. That's why I send other brothers and sisters out to do it for me, because they do it better. I do other things they can't."

By this time Gordo was feeling thoroughly sorry for himself.

"I don't think there's anything I do that's better than anyone else. I don't contribute."

"You frighten dogs better than anyone else, dogs who don't know you, that is," said Tazar. "Nobody will mess with you or with the team while you're around, and when it gets down to it you're a good fighter, even though you don't like it. This realm's safer with you in it."

"You think so?" asked Gordo.

"I do."

"Well, I suppose." Gordo was obviously pleased.

"So here's the deal," said Tazar. "We'll hunt it, and you eat it. How's that sound?"

"I think it's a deal I can live with," said Gordo with a smile.

And that was the last time anyone said anything on the subject.

12
Tazar's Secret

Life in the park was improving. The weather slowly got warmer, which made everything much easier. Not only was getting around less dangerous for the dogs, but Waggit and Lowdown also discovered on one of their foraging trips that holes had begun to appear in the ice on the Bigwater. Now they were able to drink real water again instead of chewing on icicles. Magica and Gordo were back to full health, and it seemed that the only lasting effect of their recent poisoning was to make Gordo take his new position of team security chief a bit too seriously. He was overprotective and cautious with everyone, especially Magica, even bossy on occasion. Except for Gruff, they all tolerated this good naturedly, knowing that it was just a matter of time before he forgot what he was supposed to do, and once again became the lovable bumbler that they were used to.

One morning Waggit was lying in front of the tunnel, watching Little One and Little Two play. He could see from their games that they were learning to hunt. This was the serious side to the puppies' fun, one upon which their survival would depend. He also realized how much he had changed since that fateful night when he first met Tazar. Up to that moment he had led a sheltered and protected life, something that these two puppies would never know, but which they would never miss.

Lowdown joined him and lay down by his side. Waggit hated to see how hard it was becoming for his friend to do this. Lowdown's joints were feeling the effects of aging and lack of medical care that came with the life of a park dog, but he rarely let his aches and pains affect his genial disposition.

"Look at those little devils," Lowdown said affectionately. "Don't it seem just like yesterday that you was doing the same thing yourself?" He paused and looked at Waggit. "Well, of course for *you* it *was* yesterday."

Waggit smiled. "I guess it was, but it feels like a lot longer ago than that."

"Yeah, you grow up quick around here," said Lowdown. "Come to think of it, you grow old quick too."

"You're not growing old," said Waggit, playfully nudging his friend with his nose. "You're just getting grumpier. Pretty soon you and Gruff will be agreeing with each other."

"Oh Dear Vinda!" Lowdown laughed. "If that ever happens, put me out of my misery—please!"

Just then Tazar appeared. He nodded to them as he passed.

"I'll see you guys later," he said, and then trotted off into the woods.

"I wonder where he goes every day," said Waggit.

"I doubt we'll ever know," said Lowdown.

A sudden thought occurred to Waggit.

"Why not?" he said. "Why shouldn't we know? What if I follow him and find out?"

"You'd never make it," said Lowdown. "Tazar's too smart to let himself be followed. He'd know you was there before you got to the Deepwoods."

"Hey," Waggit protested, "remember who you're talking about. It's me—the best hunter on the team. Think of all the things I've tracked without them knowing. I'm going to give it a try."

"All right," said Lowdown. "I'd tell you Tazar won't like it—but it don't matter, since he'll sniff you out faster than you sniff out a scurry."

Waggit started out in the direction that Tazar had headed and soon picked up his scent. The wind was blowing from the Deepwoods End, which not only made it easier to track Tazar, but also meant that he would be unlikely to smell Waggit if the younger dog followed far enough behind.

Within moments Waggit saw the big black dog loping casually along a wooded path. Every so often he paused to sniff at a tree or a patch of grass. He seemed unaware of Waggit's presence, and on occasion stopped to talk with a loner. If he knew he was being followed he gave no indication of it but kept going farther into the deepest and most wooded part of the park.

Tazar suddenly became more wary, quickening his stride, and looking over his shoulder, zigzagging from side to side, trying to break the scent trail that all dogs leave. He suddenly stopped and looked around him in a full circle. Fortunately Waggit knew his leader's body language quite well by now and was able to anticipate many of his movements. This allowed him just enough time to hide behind a large maple tree. He waited a few moments before looking around it. When he did, to his surprise Tazar had gone—he had simply disappeared.

Very carefully Waggit started to scout the area, doing exactly what he would if he'd lost sight of his prey on a hunt. Backward and forward he went, moving low to the ground, his nose twitching as he tried to pick up the scent again. He would get tantalizing whiffs of it and then it would vanish, so he knew Tazar was still in the area. Waggit had moved into a clump of trees when something caught his attention. He dropped to the ground and very carefully lifted his head.

Not far from him, in a bowl made from the roots of a large oak tree, were Tazar and a pretty female dog. They seemed to be hiding something that Waggit couldn't see. He moved very slowly and carefully to get a better view. There, nestled against the female's body, were two puppies, neither of them more than a few days old. Both Tazar and the female seemed absorbed in watching the litter, when suddenly Tazar lifted his head and sniffed the air. Waggit froze; he realized in a flash that in moving around to get a better view he was now upwind of the black dog, who had picked up his scent.

"Waggit," barked Tazar, "come on out. I know you're there."

Waggit lay still, his heart pounding. There would be a price to pay for this. Maybe he could get away without being seen and then deny that he had ever been in this part of the woods. He edged around the side of the trees that were protecting him. Lying flat to the ground he gingerly moved forward, but once again his tail gave him away. Wagging furiously because he was so nervous, it stood up above the low bushes that were hiding his body, and couldn't have been more noticeable had a flag been tied to it.

"Waggit," came Tazar's booming voice, "if there's one tail in this world that I would recognize anywhere, it's yours. No use hiding; I know you're there."

Sheepishly, if that's possible for a dog, Waggit stood up and walked toward the leader. As he got closer his head got lower and his ears flatter. Tazar looked at him sternly.

"Waggit, how'd you find me here?" he asked.

"I tracked you," said Waggit in a low voice.

"You did what?" Tazar was incredulous.

"Tracked you," replied a very miserable Waggit.

"All the way from camp?"

"Yeah." Waggit's voice was barely a whisper by now.

"Brother, you are one good tracker," said Tazar in a mixture of disbelief and admiration. "I never suspected you were there for one moment, and I always know when I'm being tracked. At least I thought I did."

"If I was that good a tracker we wouldn't be having this talk now," said Waggit, "'cause I would've been out of here."

"Yes," agreed Tazar, "that's the trouble with mistakes. You make just one and all the good stuff's gone. But still you tracked me all this way, and that's impressive."

Waggit began to realize that Tazar wasn't angry at being followed, but was quite proud of the fact that the young dog had managed to do it.

"So why did you want to follow me in the first place?" Tazar inquired.

"Well," said Waggit, "you've been spending so much time away from the team lately, and I was just curious about what you did."

"What did you think I was doing?" asked Tazar.

"Lowdown, Cal, and Raz said you were getting intelligence about the park, and that's why you know what's gonna happen before it does. Gruff said it was because you needed to get away from us all from time to time, as he would if he wasn't feelin' so poorly."

"And you, Waggit?" asked Tazar. "What did *you* think?"

"I didn't know," said Waggit. "That's why I was curious."

Tazar said nothing but just stood and looked at Waggit. The younger dog could feel no hostility coming from him, in fact quite the opposite. He felt Tazar's warmth, a fondness for him like a father feels toward a gifted son.

"Come here," Tazar eventually said. "I want you to meet someone."

He led Waggit to the bowl at the foot of the tree where the female dog and her puppies lay. The female looked up as they approached, and you could see that she was very shy, even shier than Alona.

"Waggit, I'd like you to meet Solosa," said Tazar.

"Very pleased to meet you," said Waggit politely.

The female dog said nothing but kept her eyes fixed on Tazar.

"She's my mate," he said, "and these are my"—he corrected himself—"our puppies."

Waggit looked from Tazar to Solosa and to the little bundles of fur that lay happily next to their mother. It was a lot of information to take in all at once.

"So now you see why I've been spending so much time away from the team," said Tazar. "I've got other responsibilities now."

"Does that mean you're leaving us?" asked Waggit—somewhat selfishly maybe, but that had been his biggest fear all along.

"Leave you?" said Tazar. "Why would I leave my team? Of course I won't leave you. You're my family just as much as these little ones and this beautiful dog."

Solosa really was beautiful; there was no denying that.

"Why doesn't she come and join the team?" asked Waggit.

"Solosa was born in the park. She's been a loner all her life. No way could she become a team dog now. We've agreed that when the little ones are old enough they'll come to the team, but it'll be a few risings before that happens," Tazar replied.

"Why didn't you tell us about her and about the puppies?" asked Waggit.

"What was the first thing you said when you found out? You said, 'Are you leaving us?' The rest of the team would have had exactly the same response," Tazar replied. "And not everyone would have believed me when I said that there was no way I would leave you all."

He paused for a moment.

"In fact, little brother," he continued, "it's probably best if they still don't know until the puppies are big enough to join us; so you and I have a secret to keep."

Waggit didn't know how he felt about this. His initial reaction was pride at sharing something so important with the leader, something that nobody else knew. But then he realized that keeping it secret would mean not being entirely honest with Lowdown and the others. This made him very uncomfortable, for Lowdown and he had no secrets, and that was what made them so close.

Tazar could see all this in Waggit's face.

"You know," he said, "the job of a leader is to keep the team safe, provided for, and happy, and sometimes what they don't know is more important to their happiness than what they do. Now I don't lie to the team—never have and never will—but there are times when it's best not to tell everyone everything, and this is one of them. So you've got to keep it a secret—just for now."

Waggit thought for a bit and then made up his mind.

"Okay," he said, "I can do that."

He looked around the area where Solosa and the puppies lived. In many ways the Deepwoods End was the prettiest part of the park, because it was the wildest. Few humans ever came here, even in the summer when there were streams running and birds singing. It was as if the city, with its noise and smells and traffic, was another world away.

"Why don't you want to live here with them?" he asked Tazar.

"Well, you know, sometimes it seems like a wonderful idea," the black dog replied, "but in my heart of hearts I know it wouldn't work. I've been a team dog as long as I've been in the park, same as Solosa's always been a loner. We live different lives because we've got different natures. I love the team. I love waking up in the morning and knowing everyone's around. I love laughing with them and caring for them when they're sick or upset. I love calming them down, or jazzing them up. To me, being a team dog is a bigger life than being a loner, but Solosa doesn't see it that way. It's just the way you are, I guess, just what you're used to. In the end you have to stay true to your nature."

Waggit remained with the two dogs and their puppies for a little while longer. The puppies were still too young to play, and although they were cute, he didn't find them very interesting. Tazar and Solosa seemed to want to be together, so he said his good-byes and headed back toward the Risingside. As he walked back along the paths that led to his home he thought about what Tazar had said, and wondered what his own true nature was.

The first dog he met when he got back to the tunnel was Lowdown. He looked up and laughed his wheezing laugh.

"Did he sniff you out?" he asked. "I bet he did. He sniffed you out, didn't he?"

"Yeah," admitted Waggit, "he sniffed me out."

"I knew he would," said the delighted Lowdown. "That Tazar, he's so smart, ain't no dog could track him down without him knowing it, not even you, and you're good."

It was true that Tazar had picked up his scent when he moved upwind to see better, so Waggit felt he hadn't lied to his friend. It was like Tazar had said, there are occasions when it's best not to tell everyone everything.

13

Captured

Spring was in the air. You could feel it and smell it. Even the humans could smell it.

As the days became longer and warmer, the pace of life in the park picked up. Now instead of hurrying, shoulders hunched and collars pulled up around their ears, the humans strolled at a more leisurely pace. For the dogs, life became a bit easier, and yet more difficult at the same time. Because there were more people around, there was more food, but also more rangers, or so it seemed. As far as they were concerned, getting the park ready for spring included not only blowing away the dead leaves with noisy, smelly machines, but also taking a much more aggressive approach to any dog off a leash. A couple of loners who had ventured too close to the Skyline End had already been captured, and Cal and Raz had to make an undignified escape while foraging near the Bigwater when they were chased by a female worker brandishing a spade.

The big question was, What would happen to the restaurant in the park now that Tashi's team no longer existed? The Tazarians had seen neither hide nor hair of Tashi and his evil lieutenant, Wilbur. It was assumed that the restaurant and its magnificent, often overflowing Dumpsters would be handled on a first-come, first-served basis by the rest of the dogs, now that it was no longer in anyone's realm. It was going to require very fine timing. You couldn't get there too early, while the restaurant workers were still filling the containers, but if you arrived too late all of the good stuff would be gone.

Waggit still thought they should've moved to the Goldenside and taken over Tashi's realm for themselves, but Tazar continued to reject this idea. For one thing they had not been able to find a shelter there that was as safe, dry, and comfortable as the tunnel, although Waggit and Lowdown had spent many hours looking for one. Tazar also felt that the restaurant should be available to all of the dogs in the park, not hoarded by one group or another. In his opinion there was more than enough food to go around, and that the huge amount they had found in Tashi's stash was evidence of his greed. Waggit, remembering the many days of the recent past when they had no food at all, didn't agree. To him it was good planning on Tashi's part to have prepared for the lean winter days.

As for the rest of the team, Little One and Little Two had grown enormously since they had been adopted. They were obviously going to be big dogs, but nobody had bothered to rename them, and Waggit suspected that they never would. It would soon be time to send them out on their first hunts to test the skills that they had developed at play. Lowdown was feeling much better with the warmer weather, his joints no longer as creaky as they had been during the bitter cold. However, Gruff was predicting a wet spring according to the feelings in *his* bones. Alicia spent most of her time washing her coat with her elegant tongue and generally preening herself—for what, nobody knew, because she rarely left the tunnel; when she did she looked magnificent. Actually she was the dog that could move most freely through the park, with the least amount of harassment; she was such a fine and expensive-looking creature that everyone who saw her assumed that she must have an owner. This would have been a great benefit to the team had she ever condescended to go anywhere on their behalf, but when asked to do anything, she either decided that the request was beneath her or she was too tired. Why they all put up with her behavior they were not quite sure, but that was the way she had always been, and she was a kind of fixture now.

Alona was the opposite of Alicia in almost every way. Had she been on a leash led by the mayor she would still look like a park dog. She moved like one, always avoiding open spaces, hurrying into the thick undergrowth. Her coat was always matted and covered with leaves or bits of twig, and she was suspicious of everyone and everything except her fellow team members, whom she had come to love. She was really halfway between a team dog and a loner, and would often disappear for days at a time, then return and sleep from sunrise to sunset. She was a good, although not a great, hunter, but her biggest contribution to the team was the information she brought back from the far reaches of the park. Although loners lived solitary lives, they nevertheless had a strong network among themselves, and surprisingly were the most terrible gossips. It was through Alona that the team got most of its news about park happenings.

Magica and Gordo had fully recovered from their near-death experience, which, in a strange way, had brought them closer together, and they were rarely seen apart. As the team had predicted, Gordo no longer played the role of security officer. Either he had forgotten or become bored with it. The other two dogs who were rarely apart were Cal and Raz, the perpetual adolescents, who goaded each other into taking the biggest risks and were always courting disaster. They were the best scavengers on the team because they would always get closer to the food vendors or the customers outside the snack bar than the other dogs dared. On many occasions they had avoided capture by inches. Although they teased each other with accusations of cowardice or weakness, in reality they were the two animals who were most closely bonded;

they would have died to protect each other.

Tazar continued to be the dominating presence in the team and the undisputed leader. He was spending less time away now that his puppies were a little bigger, but their existence and that of Solosa was still a secret. Alona had picked up a snippet of news about Solosa's new family, but not who the father was.

So this was the team at the beginning of spring. They were a tight-knit and strongly bonded group, well led, well housed, and looking forward to the summer months, when they would be well fed. They faced the future with optimism, blissfully unaware how short-lived their cheery confidence was destined to be.

The problem began when Waggit and Lowdown were walking along some paths that led to the Deepwoods. They were supposed to be foraging, but they were just enjoying being together and feeling the balmy breeze and the warmth of the sun. On days like this being a free dog in the park seemed to both of them the best possible life. It was amazing how quickly the hardships of winter vanished from memory with the mildness of spring. As they sauntered along talking about this and that, they suddenly heard the sound of a human singing. It was a woman's voice, and it would stop every so often while she took a mouthful of something to eat. They could smell the food that was her meal—some kind of meat, that much they knew. They were surprised that she was in this part of the park, because humans hardly ever came here even in the height of summer, let alone this early in the year. Neither dog had eaten much that day, or even the day before, and they were both hungry.

"Let's go and see if she drops some," whispered Waggit.

"Okay, but be careful," said Lowdown.

"Aren't you coming too?" asked Waggit.

"No, I'm too old and slow," said Lowdown. "You go and see, and if you get some bring it back here."

Waggit thought that Lowdown used the "old and slow" excuse a little too often, but he let it go this time. Very carefully he edged toward the sounds and smells under the cover of some bushes. Then suddenly he saw her; she was sitting crossed-legged on a rock with a package of sandwiches by her side, thick pastrami sandwiches, fat with layer upon layer of thin, sliced meat. In one hand she held a piece of paper with strange markings on it. It was a sheet of music, but

Waggit didn't know that, and neither did he care. All he could see was the meat, and he could feel the drool starting to run out of his mouth.

He was so focused on it that he forgot that the leaves on the bushes under which he crouched were still young and not fully formed. They weren't doing as good a job of hiding him as he had hoped. The woman suddenly looked up and caught sight of him.

"Why hello, little fellow," she said in a pleasant voice. "Who are you, and where did you come from?"

Waggit froze, his mind quickly planning his escape.

"Don't be scared," she said. "I won't hurt you."

Waggit of course could not understand anything she said. All he could think of was the piece of sandwich in her hand and the pastrami that overflowed its edges. She saw him looking at the food.

"Do you want some?" she asked, holding out her hand. "Here."

Waggit had been told too many stories by Tazar and others of the ways that humans tried to trap you, and there was no way he was going to go closer. On the other hand he was mesmerized by the smell of the meat. When he didn't move, the woman took the pastrami out of the bread and threw it toward him. It landed about a foot away from his nose, the smell overpowering him, and he couldn't resist. He rushed forward, snatched it in his mouth, and ran back to Lowdown. They divided it up pretty much equally between them, although Waggit did get slightly more, which was only right, considering that he was the bigger dog and he was the one who got it in the first place.

"Boy, that was good," whispered Lowdown. "It's a pity that's all there was."

"I'll go back and see if she does it again," Waggit quietly replied.

"Be careful," said Lowdown. "It might be a trap."

"Don't worry," Waggit said.

Slowly and carefully, he went back to the same spot, all the while looking out for anything that was suspicious.

"Why, you're back," said the woman. "Was that good? Ready for some more?"

Waggit lay there prepared to run at the first sign of trouble. Then the woman took all the meat from one half of a sandwich and tossed it at him. This time she threw it too hard, and it hit him full in the face.

"Oops." She laughed. "Sorry!"

Waggit didn't care. The only thing he was worried about was collecting all the pieces as quickly as possible and then making his escape. He ran triumphantly back to Lowdown, holding his head high, the pastrami flopping up and down.

"My oh my," said Lowdown admiringly when he saw all the meat in Waggit's jaws, "that's way too much for us to eat here. We have to take that back to the team."

Waggit knew that he was right. It *was* too much to eat on the spot, and so they started back toward the tunnel, where they would add it to the communal meal that night.

The following day Lowdown was feeling stiff and achy and told Waggit that he thought he would stay in the tunnel and rest. Cal and Raz invited Waggit to join them instead, but he politely refused. He had a hunch that the woman might be there again. There was no reason to think that she would be, but in the time that he had lived in the park the young dog had come to rely on his instincts and had found that they were rarely wrong.

Sure enough, as he got closer to the spot where they had met the day before, he could hear her singing again, only this time there was no evidence that she was eating. There were no pauses in her song, no noises made by her chewing, and no muffled notes. There was, however, a strong smell of meat again, and a delighted smile when she saw him.

"Well hello," she said. "You're back. I hoped you would be."

He lay there, tense, but not quite as tense as yesterday, his eyes focused on a large kielbasa sausage that lay on the rock by her side.

"Looks good, doesn't it?" she said and broke off a piece, holding it out in her hand for him to take.

He was still wary of going too close to her, even though she seemed nice enough. He was moving slowly toward her when he heard a twig snap nearby. He leapt back, his heart pounding, but nothing happened. It was probably a raccoon or a squirrel breaking a branch as it went by, but it was enough to make him stay exactly where he was.

"You still don't trust me, do you?" said the woman. "I'm okay, honestly."

She threw the piece of sausage to him and this time it landed perfectly, right between his paws. He wolfed it down without moving.

"Wow," she said, "you *are* hungry. I wonder who you belong to? You don't have a collar on."

Waggit didn't understand any of her words, but he did understand that there was still most of a kielbasa left next to her on the rock.

"Well, my little friend, you can have all of this," she offered, picking it up, "but you're going to have to come and get it."

She held the sausage out, and Waggit waited for her to throw it, but she didn't.

After a while she said, "Come on. Come and take it. I won't hurt you."

He moved forward a couple of paces.

"That's right," she coaxed, "come on."

He crept a little closer; she didn't move; again a few inches nearer the sausage; again she didn't move. Finally he could stand it no longer and ran forward, snatched the food out of her hand, and ran back to the tunnel as fast as his legs could carry him.

When he arrived, panting and out of breath, he dropped the sausage onto the evening's supper pile. Lowdown looked at it and turned to Waggit.

"It's from that Upright again, isn't it?" he said.

"No," said Waggit, "I just found it."

"Are you sure?" asked Lowdown.

"Absolutely sure," said Waggit.

He had no idea why he lied to his best friend, but he did. Something inside him wanted to keep the woman for himself; it wasn't a plan or anything as complicated as that, but just a feeling that this was what he should do.

It was the same instinct that told him to go back the next day by himself, and then the day after that, and the one after that. Each time she was there, sitting on the same rock in the same cross-legged position and singing. And each day she had some delicious treat. She knew he liked meat, and the food she brought was always different from the day before. He became more trusting with every encounter, and by the third day he allowed her to stroke him and tickle him under the chin, both of which she did very well.

On the sixth day he turned up at the same time, but there was no sound of singing as he approached their usual meeting place. He continued more cautiously, keeping beneath the bushes as much as he could. She was nowhere to be seen. Maybe he was too early or too late, or maybe she was. He thought he had better wait for a while in case she turned up. As he lay there his nose started working. He was definitely getting a faint scent of meat. Maybe she had turned up early and, when she saw that he wasn't there, had left a package by the rock.

He decided to get up to investigate, and he approached the place from which he thought the smell was coming. Suddenly something grabbed the loose flesh at the back of his neck and whisked him off the ground. He was suspended in midair, his legs flailing around desperately, trying to get a grip on something.

"Got you," yelled a voice triumphantly. "Got you, you little devil."

Out of the corner of his eye Waggit could see the dreaded green material that was part of the uniform that the park rangers wore. He bared his fangs, frantically trying to get away. But his captor's grip was too strong, and holding the clawing animal at arm's length he quickly walked toward the road. Parked just around the corner was the truck that every park dog feared, the one that took you to the Great Unknown, from which no dog ever returned.

14

Terror in the Great Unknown

The truck lurched, bumped, and rattled its way through the city. Inside, one to a cage, were Waggit and three other terrified dogs. One of them, a small animal of very mixed breeding, whimpered constantly. There were no windows and the only light came from a small dome in the roof that shed an unfriendly, yellowish glow on the interior. For each of the creatures it was a nightmare come true.

It seemed as if they were driving forever. Waggit wondered if this would be where he would spend the rest of his life. Maybe the Great Unknown was actually the back of the truck. Finally the vehicle braked sharply and came to a halt. Waggit heard the sounds of gates being rolled back. The truck started up again, moved forward a short distance, and then stopped once more.

The back doors were flung open, and standing there were four men, each wearing blue coveralls and thick, heavy leather gloves. Because Waggit had been the last dog captured he was the first one taken out. One of the men opened the metal cage and slipped a chain collar attached to a leash over Waggit's head. He then took him by the scruff of his neck and roughly pulled him out and dropped him on the ground.

Waggit looked around and saw a courtyard surrounded by gloomy old industrial buildings. He was pulled toward a door in the wall of one of them. It was strange to be back on a leash again after so many months without even a collar. He struggled, trying to get it off, but the more he pulled the tighter the chain got.

As the man opened the door a wave of noise hit Waggit, so loud it was almost physical, and he was led into a huge room filled with metal cages like those in the truck, only bigger. In each was a dog, and almost every one was either barking or howling. He counted dozens of them as he was led past one sad face after another. The fear that he could feel coming from them made the hair on the back of his neck stand up. It was the scariest, most unhappy place that he had ever been.

They finally came to an empty cage with its door open, and the man shoved Waggit in, took off the chain, and then shut the door with a clang as he left. There was nothing inside except for a bowl with water in it; the only place to sleep was on the cold steel floor, but sleep was the last thing on his mind. To his right a skinny dog was standing on its hind legs, barking furiously and scratching at the wire, trying to get out. To his left was a medium-size, depressed-looking hound, whose droopy jowls had spread out on the floor where he lay.

"Who are you?" barked Waggit at the top of his voice, trying to be heard over the noise.

The hound didn't move except for his eyes, which rolled in Waggit's direction in a mournful stare. After several minutes the barking finally died down.

"No point in trying to make yourself heard over that din," the hound said, still without lifting his head.

"I'm Waggit," said Waggit. "Who are you?"

"The name's Bloomingdale, like the store," said the dog.

Waggit didn't know what Bloomingdale's or indeed any store was, so he let this comment pass.

"Where did they get you?" he asked instead.

"About a block from my house," Bloomingdale said.

"What do you mean?" asked Waggit.

"What part of 'a block from my house' do you not understand?" he replied somewhat testily. "I was on my way back to my house when they picked me up."

"You mean you lived in a house with Uprights?" Waggit said.

"Of course," said Bloomingdale. "Where else would you live?"

"So why didn't they stop the Ruzelas from taking you?" Waggit was now confused.

"I was by myself," explained Bloomingdale. "I found a way of opening the back door to get out. Between you and me," he continued confidingly, "I need to get out of the house from time to time. They're a bit over-protective, and a dog needs some freedom."

Had he been speaking a foreign language his words could not have been more mystifying to Waggit. All of the dogs in the park had exactly the opposite experiences with human beings. The best treatment they had received was neglect; the worst was cruelty.

"And how about you?" inquired Bloomingdale. "How did you come to be in this mess?"

"I did something I should never have done," replied Waggit, with an edge of bitterness in his voice. "I trusted an Upright."

"Oh," sighed Bloomingdale despairingly, "and he let you down?"

"She, actually," said Waggit, "and she didn't just let me down, she tricked me."

And with that the two animals fell silent, each thinking about the injustice and treachery in the world.

There were many things about being in the Great Unknown that were terrible—the fear of not knowing what was going to happen next; the boredom of hours spent doing nothing; the discomfort of the metal cages. But Waggit hated the lights most, because they were on all the time. As a park dog he had lived by nature's clock; it was either night or day. Here you couldn't tell which it was, except for the daily exercise period when he and about ten other dogs would be led into the yard and walked around on leashes.

Mealtimes were also a way of knowing that another day had passed, when a metal bowl containing some sloppy canned food would be pushed into the cage. Bloomingdale often didn't eat his, complaining about its quality, but for Waggit it was fine. He had eaten far worse during the winter, and for him having food on a regular basis was a novelty.

There were two other grim ways of knowing both that time was passing and that time was short. Once a day those dogs who had been there the longest would be led one by one out of the room and through a door at the far end. Nobody knew where they were going, but everyone knew that they never came back. Often the departing creatures would look over their shoulders as if to get one last glance at the life they were leaving. This always happened just after mealtime, and the dogs who were to leave that day knew it, because they would be passed over as the food was handed out. Everyone was in no doubt that one day they would be the ones who would get no food.

And every day more dogs were brought in. When this happened all the dogs would howl and bark to greet the newcomers. These were not sounds of joy, but of hopelessness, and each time that it happened it so upset Waggit that he would shake with fear and loneliness. He longed to see Lowdown's cheery face, or even Gruff's grumpy one.

When a human being who was not one of the workers was led into the room, he or she would walk solemnly past each cage. The person would sometimes pause hesitantly in front of one of the dogs, frown and shake his or her head. Then suddenly there would be a cry from both the human and a dog, and the rest of the inmates would know that some lucky soul had been reunited with his owner. This would set off another round of barking and howling, but this time they were whoops of rejoicing. It gave them all hope. But not Waggit. To be rescued by your owner meant that you had to have one in the first place.

The worst day for him was the one on which Bloomingdale was given no food. Waggit had grown fond of the gloomy guy with his bleak view of the world, and when no bowl was placed in his cage they both looked at each other sorrowfully.

"Oh well," said Bloomingdale. "I suppose it was bound to happen sooner or later."

"I don't understand," said Waggit, "why your Uprights didn't come to get you. If they wanted to protect you so badly, why wouldn't they look for you?"

"Who knows?" said Bloomingdale. "They were very private. Kept to themselves. Maybe it was too much bother, or maybe they didn't want to make a fuss. In the end the reason isn't important. The fact of the matter is that they didn't come, and now it looks like I've run out of time."

There was nothing Waggit could say to this, and so the two just waited until the inevitable happened. Shortly after the food distribution one of the workers came up to Bloomingdale's cage, opened it, and slipped a chain collar around his neck. Bloomingdale gave Waggit one last, mournful look.

"So long, pal," he said, "and good luck!"

And then, with his head held high, he walked briskly off to whatever fate awaited him on the other side of the door. Waggit felt as if someone with very cold fingers had squeezed his heart, and to lie there on the hard floor and look at the empty space next to him was almost more than he could bear. It was unfair. Bloomingdale was a good dog, a threat to no one. Beneath his gloomy exterior he cared for other dogs and, even after his experiences, held no bitterness toward humans. All he had wanted was a little freedom, something that Waggit could certainly understand, and for this he was to be punished with—who knew what, but whatever it was, it wasn't good. Waggit also realized that it would soon be his day to get no food. He had come into the Great Unknown only a short time after Bloomingdale, so it couldn't be far off. He let out a long, sorrowful howl of despair.

But the worst day miraculously turned into the best. Not long after Bloomingdale's departure, Waggit's ears pricked up at the sound of a great commotion from the other side of the entry door. Suddenly it was flung open and in walked the woman from the park. One of the workers was trying to stop her.

"Ma'am, you can't come in!" he said. "You haven't filled out the necessary paperwork."

"Oh, phooey on your paperwork. I've lost my dog and I intend to look for him in here," she said, with the air of a woman who was determined to get her own way.

And she strode in, leaving the worker behind. He could only make a gesture of helplessness and follow her. She walked quickly up and down the first row of cages, and then turned toward Waggit's.

"That's him," she said, pointing to Waggit. "That's my dog. Release him at once."

"Are you sure that's the one?" asked the worker. "Because he's not barking in recognition, and come to think of it neither are any of the others. They always bark when somebody comes to claim one of them."

"He's a very reserved dog," said the woman, "never been one for showing much emotion."

At first Waggit wondered who they were talking about, looking around to see which dog it was that she was claiming. Then he realized that it was him.

"Suit yourself," said the worker. "I don't much care if he's your dog or not. He's out of here tomorrow, one way or the other, so you're saving us a bit of bother. But you still have to do the paperwork before I can release him to you."

"Oh, for goodness sake, get me your stupid paperwork and let's be done with it," she said.

The worker scurried off through the entry door to get the necessary forms. While he was gone the woman looked at Waggit and winked.

"Don't worry, kid," she said. "We'll spring you from here in no time."

The man returned with a clipboard and a pen, and

the woman scribbled a few words down and signed at the bottom of the form with a flourish. She also handed some money to the worker, who counted it and clipped it to the board. He produced a leash and collar, opened the door to the cage, and attached the collar to Waggit. Then he was led out and given into the care of the woman, and together they walked through the yard, out of the large metal front gates, and into freedom.

Outside at the curb was a yellow taxi that she had told to wait while she went inside. She flung open the door and lifted Waggit onto the backseat.

"You can't bring that dog in here," objected the driver.

"It's okay," said the woman, "he's a service dog."

"Oh yeah," said the driver, "and what kind of a service would that be?"

"It's a service that he performs for me," she replied. "He keeps me calm enough to give taxi drivers large tips."

She slammed the door, and the cab drove off with Waggit inside, on his way to his new life.

15

A New Life

The cab pulled up in front of an apartment building. It was like those that Waggit had seen from the park, only not as grand. When they got out of the vehicle they went up to the front door, which the woman opened with a key and then led them both into a simple lobby. At the far end was a metal door with a button beside it. The woman pushed it and waited; Waggit assumed she was waiting for someone to let them in. After a few moments the door slid open and she stepped into a tiny, empty room with no windows.

Waggit didn't like the look of it, and he pulled against the leash to prevent himself from being dragged inside. He still didn't trust the woman and was sure that she had been in cahoots with the ranger who had captured him. He had left the Great Unknown with her because he really didn't have much choice. It seemed to him that even if she wasn't trustworthy it was a whole lot better than staying behind. He didn't like the little room, however, and imagined all sorts of terrible things that could happen there.

"Well, what do you know," said the woman. "You've never been in an elevator before, have you? It's okay, there's nothing here to be frightened about."

Although he couldn't understand her words, her voice sounded kind and caring, and part of him wanted to believe it. Hesitantly he stepped forward, and as he did the door started to close. The woman stopped it with a sharp slap of her hand, which made him jump. She crouched down to his level and looked him in the eyes.

"Come on," she said in a calm, soft voice. "I won't let anything hurt you. I promise."

Once again her tone and manner seemed genuine enough, and the barriers of his mistrust lowered a little.

Trembling all over, he went into the elevator. The door closed behind them, and then, as if confirming all his fears, it started to shake, and there was a terrible grinding noise as it began to move. Waggit was cursing himself for being a fool when the door opened again. They got out and turned to the right, walked past several doors, and then stopped at one, which she opened with a key, and they went inside.

She led him into a large, airy room with big windows that overlooked the back of another building. In one corner was a grand piano, which, of course, meant nothing to Waggit. Along one side of the room was a small, open kitchen, which did mean something to him because of all the food smells emanating from it. Scattered throughout the room were cushions, lots of brightly colored cushions, on the furniture, on the floor, even on the closed lid of the piano. It was a very bright and cheerful room. The woman bent down and removed the leash.

"Well, kid," she said, "this is it. This is home. What do you think?"

As if to answer her question he started to walk around sniffing everything. There were a couple of interesting food spills, some areas that smelled of the same perfume she had been wearing when he first met her in the park, and one or two places that had a musty, vaguely masculine aroma. When he exhausted all the possibilities he looked up at her, panted, and sat down.

"Does that mean it's okay?" she said. "We'll assume it does." She thought for a moment, and then said, "I bet you're thirsty. Stress always makes me as dry as a bone."

She went into the kitchen, found a rather chipped bowl, filled it with water, and put it down on the floor. Waggit circled it suspiciously, sniffed it a couple of times, and after deciding that it probably wasn't poisoned, drank enthusiastically.

"And talking of bones," she continued, "what do you like to eat?"

The answer was almost anything, but being a dog he couldn't tell her that.

"I'll go to the supermarket later and see what I can find," she said, "but in the meantime I think I might have something to tide you over."

She went to the refrigerator, burrowed around in it for a few moments, and with a cry of "I thought so!" came back with a large piece of grilled chicken breast in her hand. She put it on the kitchen floor, and Waggit pounced on it. He had been so upset about Blooming-dale that he hadn't eaten the food the worker had put in his cage that morning. Now he attacked the meat ravenously.

"Well," said the woman, "I guess chicken's on the menu."

When he had finished eating, he suddenly felt tired. It had been a distressing and confusing day, and now he was so weary that it overcame all the fear and suspicion he had. There was a thick, colorful rug in the middle of the room, and on this he turned around a couple of times and lay down. He could feel his eye-lids getting heavy with drowsiness. The woman came over to him and gently stroked him behind the ears.

"That's right," she said, "you lie down there." She stretched out beside him. "You gave me a pretty good runaround before I found you," she continued. "When you didn't turn up for a couple of days I thought you must've found someone else to feed you, but then a friend told me that the park rangers had been trapping stray dogs and taking them to the pound. The trouble was I didn't know which pound, and yours was the third one I went to. There are so many dogs it's heartbreaking, and they're all so beautiful I wanted to take every one of them home. But you—I don't know what it is, but there's something about you; you're special, and I'm glad I found you."

She might as well have saved her breath, for Waggit was fast asleep.

When he awoke it was with a start. For a moment he had no idea where he was, and his heart was pounding with anxiety. His first thought was that he had to get back to the team, but exactly how he wasn't sure. For the moment he was trapped in this room with the woman, and while it was much more comfortable than the Great Unknown, he still had no idea what would happen next. His memories of the first humans that he lived with were dim by now, but being in a room such as this was enough to make him uncomfortable. Having been abandoned once, he would never completely trust humans again.

"You're back in the land of the living I see," said the woman when she noticed that he had woken up. He eyed her warily, his body tense, ready to run. She had been straightening up cushions and humming to music that was coming out of a machine on one of the bookshelves. Dogs have strange feelings about music. They can't make it, can't sing or play instruments, but they find it very soothing, even though certain notes make them howl. This music, however, didn't have any of those notes. It was a sad sound made by a single stringed instrument and it calmed him down a little. She watched him cock his head toward the machine from which it came. "You should like that," she said. "It's Bach."

Instead of going to the supermarket for his food, she decided to go to a large pet store nearby. One of the benefits of this change of plan was that Waggit could go with her, because the store allowed "well-mannered pets" to accompany their owners inside. It was here that Waggit first encountered dogs under the control of humans. The woman and he were coming around the end of one aisle when they literally bumped into a golden retriever coming the other way.

"Oh, hi," said Waggit. "How're you doing? My name's Waggit."

"What a funny name," said the golden. "My name's Daisy. Phew, you smell bad. Did you come from the pound?"

Waggit sniffed himself. There was a strange odor coming from his coat that he hadn't noticed before.

"I was in the Great Unknown," he said to Daisy. "Is that the same as the pound?"

"I've never heard of such a pl— Oh, got to go. See you." And with that her owner dragged her off.

As they were approaching the checkout line, Waggit spotted two tiny Yorkshire terriers in little plaid raincoats, even though it wasn't raining. He went over to greet them, dragging the woman with him. As he got close they started barking furiously with a high-pitched yapping sound. He had no idea why they were so angry; he only wanted to say hello and sniff them. Once again, the human at the other end of their leashes pulled them away. He couldn't understand why humans didn't want their dogs to communicate with each other. As soon as you got a conversation going they whisked you off.

Waggit's attention was now on the cart that the woman was pushing toward the cash registers. It was overflowing with food and treats, a round squishy bed, toys, brushes and combs, bowls, vitamins, chews, a toothbrush and toothpaste, and, yes, even a raincoat, only this one was yellow. It wasn't until the store delivered everything later that afternoon that he realized it was all for him. He had no idea that you needed so many things for a civilized existence. Up until that moment his most prized possession had been a cardboard box, and he had to admit that the bed was a lot more comfortable. Surrounded by all this stuff, it occurred to him for the first time that she probably intended him to stay with her, at least for a while.

Early the following morning the woman attached his leash and took him to the elevator. He was still a little nervous about getting into it, and when the doors opened he pulled back a bit until he realized that at least he was going out this time, where there might be possibilities of escape. He had smelled the park yesterday, so he knew that it couldn't be far away.

The doors closed and they started down. They had only been inside for a few seconds when the elevator stopped again, and the doors opened one floor below. A brown and white terrier flew in, pulling a somewhat disheveled woman behind him. He almost banged into Waggit, who growled softly.

"Oh, sorry, didn't see you. How are you? My name's Jack, what's yours? What a great day. Is this not a great day? As soon as I woke up I knew it was going to be a great day. I can't wait to get out. Where are you going? I'm going to the store. We'll probably go to the park later. Did you just move in? Welcome to the building. It's a great building. You'll love it here. Lots of dogs. You'll make friends in no time. Maybe we'll get them to take us out together. Whatd'ya think?"

He said all of this in one continuous stream that left Waggit gasping for breath, something that should have happened to the terrier, but didn't. Waggit didn't know how to reply or even where to begin. Not that it made the slightest bit of difference because now Jack's entire attention was on the door.

"Come on, stupid door, open up. Can you believe this door? Takes forever. Come on, come on, let's go."

Finally the elevator came to a stop and the door opened.

"About time. Well, we're off," he said, pulling his harried owner after him. "Great to meet you. Glad to have you on board. We'll get them to arrange a play date. See you later. Have a nice day."

By the time that he had shouted out his final greeting the two of them were already across the lobby and halfway out of the front door, while Waggit and the woman had barely exited the elevator.

"That," said the woman, "is Jack. He's a little hyper, but his owner's very nice."

It was good to be outside, even on a leash. Waggit had spent so much of his life in the open that it felt more natural than the enclosed space of the apartment. He could also smell the scents left by the other dogs, and that made him feel more at ease. They walked across a wide avenue, then along a side street, and suddenly there it was—the park. His park! His tail wagged in anticipation of seeing it again. The two of them entered through a gate, crossed the drive, and were on the horse path. He realized that the direction they were taking would bring them within a short distance of the tunnel, and that maybe the team would see him. He wasn't quite sure what they could do to set him free, but at least they would know that he was alive. As they got closer he could smell them and he was tense with excitement, but the woman didn't know that this was where his former home was, and she was intent on walking by. He dug his claws into the gravel of the path to try to stop her, but she just dragged him along.

"Come on, kid," she said, "there's nothing there. Let's go."

With a heavy heart he followed her. He was so close and yet as far away as ever from being reunited with his team.

They walked for a while and then returned to the apartment. It was the third time he had gone up in the elevator, and it got a little less scary each time. Even the apartment was becoming familiar and seemed less confined. When she had taken off his leash she turned to him and said, "Breakfast?" It was a word that he didn't understand yet, but, when she poured some hard nuggets of kibble into his new metal bowl and then mixed it with brown, meaty stuff that she got out of a can, that he understood. The food she made for him was the best he had ever had in his life, and furthermore it seemed that it would be a regular event, unlike in the park, where mealtimes were haphazard at best. He emptied the bowl within seconds and then let out a gentle belch.

"Oh, very nice," the woman said with a chuckle. "I see that you haven't let go of your park manners yet."

Feeling warm and sleepy after his meal, Waggit went to the squishy bed for a nap. As he lay down the woman looked at him.

"What am I going to call you?" she asked. "I can't call you 'kid' forever."

He looked up at her and blinked, almost as if he was trying to think of a new name. Suddenly the woman had a fit of inspiration and grinned broadly. "Parker!" she said. "I'm going to call you Parker. You are my little park boy after all. Is that okay with you?"

Waggit sighed and smacked his lips a couple of times.

"Not crazy about it?" said the woman, moving over to stroke his head. "Well, tough. I think it's cute, so that's your name from now on."

16

Civilization

Waggit was getting used to life with the woman, almost without noticing it. Living with her was very pleasant. She was affectionate and paid him lots of attention; he quickly got used to regular, good-tasting food; she took him for long walks in the park each day; her apartment, although small, was comfortable and bright, and he had developed a deep attachment to his bed. Actually he was now on his second bed, the first having become a victim of an unfortunate incident.

The woman was a professional singer and sang all

the time, whether she was cooking or in the shower or even walking him down the street. The best part of her job was that she was home all day; the worst was that she was out most nights, often not returning until the early hours of the morning. The first time that this happened she had to go to a rehearsal, so she said good-bye to him while it was still light. She had left him before, to go to the store, or for similarly brief periods of time, and although he didn't like it, he knew from experience that she would come back.

As usual, he was sitting in front of the door awaiting her return. It seemed as if a long time had passed, and he was becoming more and more worried that she had abandoned him. It was also getting dark, which didn't help. The darker it got the lonelier he felt. In the last rays of the day's light he went into her bedroom. She had many clothes, and many, many shoes. She loved shoes. The closet door was open a crack, and Waggit stuck his head in. It smelled of her, and the smell was comforting. Very carefully he picked up one of the shoes in his mouth and took it back to the living room. He climbed on his bed with it and waited. It was quite dark now, but because this was the city it never got totally black; he could still see the outlines of things around the room, which somehow made it scarier. He lay there trembling, apprehensive, and feeling very forlorn.

The woman returned home from work shortly after midnight. She put the key in the lock, turned it, opened the door, and was surprised to find the apartment in complete darkness. She switched on the light, and as she did so Waggit woke up. He started to run toward her, and then looked around. The room was covered in white fluff, the stuffing from his bed, the filling that gave it the deliciously squishy feeling Waggit loved so much. Worse still, in the middle of all this debris was the woman's shoe, or at least what remained of it. It was chewed beyond recognition. In a flash Waggit remembered that in his fear he had torn frantically at the bedcover and pulled out its contents, and then he had attacked the shoe. Why he had done these things he didn't know.

As if all this weren't bad enough, it also brought back a long forgotten memory of a similar incident that happened while he was living with his first family, the one that had abandoned him in the park. On that occasion he had been beaten for his wrongdoing, and he had no reason to think that he would avoid punishment this time. He cringed against the kitchen wall, trying to make himself as small a target as possible.

When the woman saw the chaos she put her hand to her mouth and gave a little cry. Slowly she turned to Waggit.

"What happened? Why did you do this?" she said.

Waggit blinked at her. His eyes were still adjusting to the brightness.

"Of course, I forgot to leave the light on. You were frightened of being alone in the dark. Oh, you poor boy," she said. "I'm so sorry. How stupid and unthinking of me. How could I leave without turning on the light? You must have been terrified. Please forgive me. I will never do it again."

Waggit was still pressed up against the wall awaiting his punishment, but to his surprise she simply put down the bag in which she carried her music and started to clean up the mess.

The following night she went out to work again, only this time she left all the lights on and soft music playing from the machine on the bookshelf. She also left Waggit on a brand-new bed with a pair of her old socks that she used to wear around the house, and a squeaky, plastic high-heeled shoe. He spent a pleasant evening alone.

If there was one thing that mad Jack was right about, it was the number of dogs who lived in the building. It often seemed to Waggit that they outnumbered the humans. Of all of them it was Jack and a golden retriever named Polly who became his closest friends. One of the disadvantages of living with a human was that you couldn't choose your hanging-out companions but got to be with whichever dogs your owner chose. Fortunately Jack and Polly's owners were good friends of the woman, and they would often visit one another's apartments and let the dogs play while they talked and drank coffee. Polly's owner lived at street level, and when the gathering was there Jack spent most of his time on the back of a couch furiously barking at passersby on the other side of the window.

"There's another one. Look at him. Too many meals there, my friend. Got to cut back. Oh no, here comes a runner! You call that running. I can walk faster than that. Hey, hey, you, I don't like the look of you. Move on or I'll come after you. It's the mailman; here comes the mailman. I love the mailman. He's so frightened of me. Hey, mailman, I'm in here. Don't worry, I'll get you tomorrow."

This monologue would continue until Jack's owner told him to shut up and swatted him off the couch. Then he would pounce upon Polly's toys (his own were nearly all destroyed) and shake them furiously. It amused Waggit to see this play-acting, because it was what he had really done to kill the animals that he had caught in the park, and he wondered if Jack would be able to do it if his life depended upon it. He suspected he would, for the little dog seemed like a survivor.

The opposite of Jack, Polly was calm, and a good listener. She loved to hear Waggit describe his adventures and was thrilled when he told her about close calls with Ruzelas and confrontations with Tashi. For Polly these stories were fables from a different planet, not somewhere that was just a short distance from where the three of them lived. Even the language Waggit used to tell his tales was foreign. Polly and Jack had never heard of scurries, or longlegs pulling luggers, or flutters, or loners.

The feeling that they were different worlds was greatest when Waggit left the apartment and went to the park with the woman, often in the company of Polly and Jack and their owners. It seemed to him that there were two parks, the one that the team lived in and the one that other people and dogs visited. They both shared the same location, but they were very different. If your life didn't depend on it, the park was a much more welcoming place, and of course, if you were with a human, you had nothing to fear from the Ruzelas.

The greatest excitement that Waggit had now was playing with Polly when they were both off the leash. The woman took him for walks in the park at least once a day, usually up the path that the horses used, but two or three times each week they would go to an area of open lawn not far from where Lowdown had fooled him into attacking the metal statue. Early in the morning people would take their dogs to this place and let them off their leashes. There would be as many as fifteen or twenty dogs, and they would chase the balls that their owners threw, or sticks that they found in the bushes, or simply cavort and wrestle with one another.

For all her gentle nature Polly played hard, rushing constantly for balls and wrestling with Waggit, often knocking him to the ground in her enthusiasm. He didn't mind this, for she seldom hurt him, and indeed he was quite flattered that she chose to play with him over all the other dogs there. One day they were both taking a necessary break, their tongues wagging up and down as they gasped for air. Suddenly and breathlessly, she said to Waggit, "Aren't you glad you don't live here all the time?"

He had to stop and think about this. In the same way that he had been slow to admit he had been abandoned when Tazar first found him, he was equally reluctant now to believe that he would never rejoin the team. In fact the first time that he came to this place and the woman took off his leash his immediate thought had been that he could easily run back to the tunnel. He was faster than any of the humans and knew back routes and secret paths through the thickest bushes, so there was no way that he would be caught. Why he didn't do it he wasn't quite sure.

"Well," said Polly, "are you or aren't you?"

"To be honest, I don't know," he replied. "I don't feel that I live like you and Jack. My life now seems sort of temporary. On the other hand," he continued, "I suppose I always thought living with the team was temporary too."

"But you're one of us now," she said with concern. "You've been rescued. There's lots of rescued dogs here. It's nothing to be ashamed of. Don't you feel like one of us?"

Before he could answer, Jack arrived, panting from the exertion of "killing" a plastic drink cup that someone had carelessly left on the ground.

"Lots of dogs here today. Lots of dogs. I like it when there's lots of dogs. I don't know why. Somehow I feel more at home. Safer maybe. How about you? What've you two been doing? I've been hunting. Caught a cup, two soda cans, and half a pretzel."

Waggit remembered when half of a pretzel would have been dinner for two dogs, and was somewhat sorry that the overfed terrier had got there first, much as he liked him.

"Jack," said Polly, "I was just saying to Parker that he was one of us now. Don't you think?"

"Of course he's one of us. Never been more sure of anything in my life. Well, for one thing he's a dog, so that makes him one of us, and for another thing we like him. And he's certainly not one of me, because I'm short and brown and white, and while he's white, so parts of him could be one of me, he hasn't got any brown, and furthermore he's tall. And he couldn't be one of you because you're a sort of reddish brown, and he's white, as I said before, and what's more he's a boy and you're not, so if he's not one of you and not one of me he must be one of us. Stands to reason, doesn't it?"

Once again Waggit had the feeling that the oxygen was being sucked out of the air when he listened to Jack's monologue.

"Do you ever," he asked when the terrier finally finished, "answer a question with a simple yes or no?"

"Well, it depends on what you mean by yes or no. If your intention when you ask a question is to get as much . . ."

"Jack!" yelled Polly. "Stop!"

One good thing about Jack was that he would shut up when told to.

"Ah, yeah, okay, fine, whatever," he said. Even agreeing to stop talking took him more words than most animals.

The three women were ready to go home, and they gathered up their dogs, attached the leashes, and walked toward the park exit. The dogs trotted along happily together, and as they did Waggit thought more about Polly's question. He liked both her and Jack, and most of the dogs who they played with in the morning, but he wasn't sure that he felt like one of them, as

Polly had put it. However, as more time passed he wasn't sure that he felt like one of the team anymore either, and he certainly had quickly become used to the comforts of life with the woman. As he looked back on his short life it seemed to have had nothing permanent about it, but to have been a series of temporary situations. His fear was that he wouldn't ever feel like "one of us," whoever the "us" was.

When they got back to the apartment the woman took off Waggit's leash.

"Okay, Parker my boy, what would you say to a little breakfast?" she said.

At first Waggit had been quite confused when the woman called him Parker. He thought it was just another of the words that she used to get his attention, in the same way that she called him "good boy," "kid," or "buddy," and even "sunshine." Polly had to explain to him that it was his new name. Of course he knew that he was really Waggit, and as far as he was concerned always would be, but he really didn't mind what the woman called him as long as she put his bowl of kibble and meat on the floor every day.

That afternoon Waggit took another step along the path of becoming a pet. The woman put on his leash and said, "You're probably not going to like this, Parker, but we need to see if you picked up any nasty diseases before I got you."

And so they left the building and walked for several blocks until they arrived at a storefront with the words UPTOWN ANIMAL HOSPITAL painted on the window. The first thing Waggit noticed was the smell—a mixture of disinfectant and fear. He tensed his body as they entered the building.

"It's okay," said the woman. "Nothing bad's going to happen to you."

They checked in with the woman behind the counter, and then went to one of the seats that ringed the wall. In one corner of the room was a small, fluffy, white dog in a canvas carrier. It whined all the time.

"Don't let them take you to her," it yapped. "That woman should be locked up. Calls herself a doctor. She's a devil, a torturer. Let me out of here. I'd sooner be sick; I'd sooner die!"

"Take no notice of him," said a mutt sitting next to Waggit. "He's an overbred, neurotic fool. As doctors go she's perfectly fine. She'll have you back to normal in no time."

"But I'm already at normal now," said Waggit. "I feel just fine."

"Oh, what's she doing, a checkup on you?" asked the mutt. "Did you just get rescued?"

"I guess so," said Waggit, who hadn't heard the term until Polly used it earlier that day.

"Yeah," said the other dog, "I was rescued too. Nice people. Can't complain. Don't worry, all they do is look you all over, stick a couple of things in you, and then tell your owner what you already know—that there's nothing wrong with you. It's no big deal."

And indeed that was the way it turned out. A few minutes later they were taken into a small room where he was weighed. Waggit wasn't terribly happy about this, but everyone kept on telling him what a good boy he was, so he put up with it. Then in swept the doctor, who had the wonderfully appropriate name DR. CARING embroidered on her white lab coat.

"Hello, Laura," said Waggit's woman. "Nice to see you again."

"Nice to see you too, although I must say I didn't think it would be this soon," said the doctor. "How long is it since Digby went to the great kennel in the sky?"

"It's just over a month."

"Where did this one come from?" asked the doctor.

"Well, I got him from the pound," said the woman, "but I first met him in the park. He'd obviously been abandoned."

"He's cute," said the doctor, turning toward Waggit. "Let me tell you, young man," she said to him, "you have just won the dog equivalent of the lottery. This woman will spoil you to death if you're not careful, and if I'm not careful."

"I'm not that bad," said the woman.

The doctor gave her a look that said "Yeah, right!" and then bent over Waggit. The sudden movement startled him and he snarled in fear.

"Hey," said the doctor, "we'll have none of that, but since you want to show me your teeth we'll start the examination there." She lifted up his jowls to expose two lines of very white incisors.

As the mutt in the waiting room had said, the doctor prodded him, listened to his heart, and stuck needles in him, some of which took blood out, others of which put stuff in. At the end of the examination she turned to the woman.

"Well, you're in luck," she said. "He's as fit as a flea,

none of which he has, by the way, which for a stray living in the park is remarkable."

Little did she know how fanatical Tazar was about hygiene and the need for team members to take regular baths in the Deepwater.

Easy though the examination was, Waggit was glad to be out of there and rushed toward the door as they turned to leave. Without having to be told, he headed back in the direction of the apartment. The woman hurried to keep up with him.

"You have a clean bill of health," she said, "so I suppose we're stuck with each other."

Waggit wasn't listening. He had only one thing on his mind—supper! He was, after all, a three-meals-a-day dog now.

17

Waggit's Good-bye

The first time that Waggit realized he was happy, he was lying on his back having his stomach scratched. The sun was streaming through the windows, warming his fur; the bed upon which he was lying was soft and squishy; the stomach that the woman was scratching was full. Life was good; he felt safe for the first time. Of course his life was different from the one he led in the park. One of the biggest changes was the way he was now dependent upon the woman for everything. If he wanted to go out he had to wait until she took him out; she decided which dogs he would play with; he ate when she gave him food, although he had discovered that if he stared at her hard enough she usually got the message. Gone were the days when he and Lowdown would suddenly decide to wander off to the Bigwater, or when dinner depended upon what you could hunt or scavenge. Life was much more structured now, and this was the price that he paid for the happiness he was feeling.

He could only live this way because he had begun to trust the woman. He relied upon her for everything, and she had not let him down, and although he didn't fit into the life of a house dog the way that Polly and Jack did, the fit was good enough. He felt that he could finally relax and let down his defenses. The only cloud that cast a shadow on his happiness was that the team didn't know what had happened to him. He felt a responsibility as the only dog who had ever come back from the Great Unknown to tell them about his experience. And he missed them. Every time he and the woman walked along the horse path he would scour the bushes looking for one of them. There were times when he thought he saw a pair of eyes or a flash of fur, but nothing more. It worried him that his decision to stay with the woman would mean that he would never again see his friends.

The woman had been working a lot recently, and this meant that Waggit was alone at night. Although he didn't like it he was used to it now. It was during one of his nights alone that he came up with a plan. The next evening the woman got ready to leave for work, settled him on his bed, checked to see that he had an adequate amount of water in his bowl, patted him on his head, and left through the front door. It was now the middle of the summer and the day had been hot, so the air-conditioning was working in the apartment. This meant that all the windows were shut tight to keep the cool air in. However, Waggit knew that there was one window in the bathroom that she kept open a few inches. He waited for a while after she left, since it was not unusual for her to leave behind her music or cell phone and come rushing back in to retrieve the forgotten object. Sure enough, she came back in a few minutes.

"Stupid cell phone," she said, as if it were the cell phone's fault that it had been left in the kitchen. She picked it up, said good-bye to Waggit again, and rushed through the front door. When he decided that she had really gone, he went to the bathroom and, sure enough, there was an opening big enough for him to get his head through.

He climbed up onto the toilet that was under the window, after knocking the lid down with his nose. He then stuck his head through the window. The gap was too small for him to crawl through, so he went as far as he could and pushed up with all his might. At first the window didn't budge, and he thought he might have to forget the idea, but on the second heave he felt it give a little. The third time was a charm, and it went up so quickly he fell out. He landed on the metal staircase outside the window with a thump that knocked the wind out of his body for a while. He got up, caught his breath, and quickly ran down the stairs. He had a limited amount of time before the woman returned, but he also had to make sure that none of the building's residents saw him as he made his way down to street level. Or almost street level, as it turned out, for the staircase stopped at the second floor. It ended with a ladder that didn't reach the ground.

He wasn't sure what to do next. Looking down, he saw that it was obviously too far for him to jump. A cat might have made it, but Waggit had never wanted to be a cat, a species he viewed with a certain amount of contempt. He leaned against the ladder to get a better view, and suddenly to his surprise it started to slide down under his weight. He leapt back, and then realized what he had to do. Very carefully he hooked one paw around the outside of one of the rungs, and swung himself out and grabbed on to the ladder with his other three paws as best he could. With him stuck in this precarious position the ladder started to go down. He could feel himself slipping, and clung on desperately until, just a short distance from the ground, he fell. As he landed on the sidewalk below, the ladder began to go up again. It was obvious that however he was going to get back into the apartment, it wouldn't be this way.

But he would have to worry about that later. Now he must get to the park as quickly and as stealthily as possible. He chose one of the smallest and quietest roads as his route, and as an added precaution he walked slowly, pausing to sniff fire hydrants and streetlights, and looked behind him frequently as if waiting for his owner to catch up. In this way he managed to pass unnoticed by any humans until he got to the wide avenue that ran alongside the park. Standing in the shadows of a church on the corner, he waited until there was a sufficient gap in the traffic, then ran with all his might across the road and into the park.

It was exhilarating to be back on his home turf by himself, and he quickly made his way to the tunnel. As he approached it he heard a voice coming from the bushes where the sentries kept watch.

"Hold up there, friend," the voice said. "Who are you, and what do you want?"

"Who are *you*?" asked Waggit.

"I'm the one asking the questions, friend," said the voice. "And you're the one what ain't answering them."

"I'm Waggit," said Waggit.

"There's no dog here by that name," said the voice. "There used to be, but he's long gone, gone to the Great Unknown."

"No," said Waggit. "*I'm* Waggit."

"Well," said a different voice that was reassuringly familiar, "if this isn't a miracle. It *is* Waggit!" And Tazar came down the path, his tail high and his head cocked. He went up to Waggit and sniffed him all over.

"Waggity boy," he said, "welcome back. How did you make it? What happened? No, don't tell me, wait until you can tell everybody. Olang, come here!"

Tumbling out of the bushes came a very young dog who wasn't nearly as tough as his voice sounded. He scrambled clumsily down to where Tazar was standing and took his place beside him.

"This is my son, Olang," said Tazar proudly. "We're training him to be eyes and ears. He's pretty good, don't you think?"

"Well, he had me worried," admitted Waggit.

"Yeah, he's a good boy," said Tazar. "Olang," he continued, "standing in front of you is a living wonder. This is Waggit, the only animal I ever heard of who got captured, taken to the Great Unknown, and not only lived to tell the tale but has come back to tell it to us."

"Is this one of the kids who I saw you with up at the Deepwoods End?" asked Waggit.

"Yes," said Tazar. "They grow quick, don't they? I'm sad to say his sister didn't make it, but this one—he's the image of his old man, don't you think?"

Waggit didn't think so, actually, but he didn't say anything, for Tazar was so proud of what was in fact an unremarkable-looking puppy.

"I'm sorry to hear about your daughter," he said. "What happened?"

"Oh, life in the park, you know. Some make it,

others don't," said Tazar. "It's just the way it is. Come, come, let's go to the others. They will be amazed to see you, and so pleased. We were distraught when the Ruzelas got you; it hasn't been the same around here since."

The three of them went into the mouth of the tunnel; Waggit stood there and in front of him he saw the entire team. There was a stunned silence and then pandemonium broke out. Everyone licked and sniffed and nudged him; they asked question after question, no one bothering to wait for an answer before asking another one. The noise in the tunnel was deafening. As his eyes got used to the low light, Waggit suddenly saw in the back of the tunnel, lying on a pile of newspapers, his old friend Lowdown. He went over to him. Lowdown struggled to get up onto his feet, which took some time. When he finally made it, his back legs trembled. Slowly and painfully he walked up to Waggit.

"My friend, my very good friend, welcome back," he said. "We have all missed you, but no one has missed you more than me. How are you?"

"I'm well," said Waggit. "Better than you, I think. What's the matter, Lowdown?"

"Oh, just age," said Lowdown, "and unfortunately there's only one cure for that. Let me tell you, the golden years ain't as golden as they'd have you believe. But I can't complain. These good animals look after me well. I want for nothing—except maybe to run with you down by the Deepwater one more time, but I don't think that's going to happen."

"Don't you believe the old fraud," interrupted Tazar. "He goes out hunting while we're all asleep. That's why he's so fat. He'll outlive us all."

Waggit only had to look at Lowdown to realize that this was Tazar's attempt to lift his friend's spirits, and it broke his heart to see the way his friend had aged.

"You were so much better the last time I saw you," said Waggit, "and I haven't been away that long."

"Well, that's the park for you," said Lowdown. "You grow up quick here and you grow old quick too." He paused for a moment. "But, you know, I wouldn't live anywhere else."

This made Waggit feel a bit awkward given the decision that he had made to stay with the woman, but he said nothing. He looked around and saw all the faces of the team eagerly watching him, waiting to hear his story. They were all there—the Ladies Alicia,

Alona, and Magica; Cal and Raz; Little One and Little Two, both of whom were now enormous; Gordo, who was still enormous; Gruff; and Tazar himself.

"Well," Waggit said, "here's what happened to me since I was here last."

And he started to tell the story of being taken by the Ruzelas, of arriving at the Great Unknown, of Bloomingdale, of being rescued by the woman, and of his friendship with Polly and Jack. As the tale unfolded, his audience reacted in different ways. Anger and fear accompanied the capture and transportation to the Great Unknown; sadness and pride were produced by the account of Bloomingdale's stoic bravery; puzzlement and confusion seemed to be the overwhelming reaction to the story of rescue and the kindness of the woman.

"You mean she searched for you?"

"She wasn't working with the Ruzelas?"

"She just, like, wanted you to live with her?"

"She hasn't beaten you?"

They found it difficult to believe that a dog could be truly happy living with a human being. In a way it shifted the whole basis of their world; this was one of the enemy that wasn't acting like an enemy at all.

"But," said Tazar, "there was one thing she couldn't give you—freedom. Once you've tasted liberty, it's mighty hard to live a life of constraint. We may not have soft beds, we may not have fancy meals, but we bow our heads to no one."

"I have to tell you, Tazar," said Waggit, "there's not a whole lot of head-bowing going on with the house dogs, petulants, or whatever you want to call them, that I've met. I'll introduce you to Jack. You never saw a more unbowed head!"

"Well, if life with the Uprights is so good," said Tazar, "why have you come back to the park? Why not stay with your new friends? Why do you want to live here again?"

This was the moment that Waggit had been dreading. To tell them that he didn't want to live with them anymore, that he preferred living with a human, seemed to be the worst act of disloyalty, even treachery, to dogs who had been his friends and had saved his life. Even though his stomach was in knots, and his heart was racing with anxiety, he took a deep breath and prepared himself to let them know his decision.

"I don't want to live here," said Waggit. "I just wanted to come back and tell you what happened to me, and that I'm all right and not to worry."

There was a stunned silence.

It was broken after a few moments by Lowdown.

"You mean that you're leaving us again?"

"I have to, Lowdown," said Waggit. "Well, that's not true. I don't have to—I want to. I love you guys, and I owe you all more than I can ever repay, but life in the park is hard. You know that. You live with fear and uncertainty every day, and I've been given the chance to live another way. The woman loves me not because I'm a good hunter, or a fast runner, but just because I'm me. If the price I have to pay for a little peace and security is to wear a leash, then so be it."

"We love you for who you are," said Magica, "at least I do."

"I know you do," said Waggit, "and this isn't coming out at all the way I wanted it to. I'm not putting down the way you guys live. You're warm and generous and a lot of fun, and like I said, I owe you big-time. I just need to give this a try. She's a good woman, and she really cares for me."

"So be it, little brother," said Tazar in an uncharacteristically soft, low voice. "We've all got to find our own way. Maybe your way is different from ours, and then maybe it isn't. Maybe we'd all do what you're doing, given the chance."

The team instinctively knew that it was now time to say good-bye. They came up to Waggit one by one and brushed against him, sniffed him, licked him, and murmured "Good luck," or "Don't forget us," for they were truly sad to see him go. Tazar was the last one to say his farewells.

"You *are* a good hunter," he said, "and we miss you for that. But we mostly miss you because you're a fine dog. Go in peace, with our good wishes, and know that you will always have a home with us whenever you want one, for we are your family."

And with that Waggit turned toward the bright lights of the city streets. As he started back, Lowdown said to him, "I would like to walk with you one last time," and so the two friends moved off in silence, one hobbling painfully, the other walking slowly beside him. When they got to the road that runs around the inside of the park, they stopped, and Lowdown turned to him.

"I never had a friend as good as you, Waggit," he said, "and I never will. You're a special dog, so no wonder the woman wants you to live with her. No way I can blame her for that. Make sure she takes care of you, and make sure you give her the love that she deserves. And don't forget me."

"I'll never forget you, Lowdown," said Waggit, shocked at the very idea, "and besides, we come into the park all the time, so I might see you again soon."

"No," said Lowdown, "this is the last time we'll meet, make no mistake about that, but carry me in your heart and I will carry you in mine."

The old dog turned and painfully headed back in the direction of the tunnel without looking back. Waggit, for his part, shot out of the park and across the avenue, barely looking where he was going. Cars screeched to avoid him, horns blaring. He raced along the streets back to the apartment, not just because he wanted to get back before the woman returned from work, but also because the act of running seemed to lessen the ache that he felt inside him. He had made his decision, and he thought it was the right one, but he was learning that sometimes the right decision can feel like the wrong one.

Happy Ending

By the time he got back to the apartment building he was out of breath, and out of ideas as to how to get back inside. He knew that the fire escape he had used to get out was not going to be his way in. Even if the ladder was down as far as it went, there was still a gap between it and the ground. Furthermore dogs are not good at climbing ladders; it was one thing to hang on for dear life as it went down, but quite another to get enough of a grip on each rung to climb up. Even if he did, how was he going to climb in the window? He was still sore from the tumble when he'd made the trip in the opposite direction.

There were two mailboxes just to the left of the building's entryway, and he hid between these in order to gather his thoughts and consider his options. The problem with options was that he didn't seem to have any, apart from staying wedged there until the woman appeared. Like all dogs he had a very poor sense of time, and he had no idea whether the wait would involve minutes or hours. It was at that moment when he heard voices coming from the building's hallway. Two people, a man and a woman, were leaving, laughing and talking loudly. They had pulled the door open very wide, and now it was slowly closing.

Timing it nicely, Waggit darted through the opening just before the door shut, and into the lobby. It smelled, as usual, of the strange water that the human who cleaned it used, but, more importantly, it was empty. He stood in front of the elevator, wondering what to do next. If he got up on his hind legs and stretched his front paws as high as they would go, he could just reach the button that the woman pressed to open the doors, and as he pushed against it they immediately slid apart. He scurried into the elevator and sat, waiting for them to close again.

When they did he continued to sit, waiting for the elevator to move, but it didn't budge. Then he remembered that you had to push buttons inside the car to make it go, but which was the correct one? He had no idea. Then it occurred to him that he didn't have to choose just one. Why not hit all of them? As the door opened on each floor he would surely recognize something that would lead him home.

So that's what he did. The task was complicated by the fact that he couldn't reach the top row, however much he stretched up on his back legs, but he didn't worry about this. He was pretty certain that he and the woman didn't live in the top part of the building; he remembered that when he made his journey down the fire escape earlier that night it didn't seem to be very high up.

The elevator stopped at the second floor and Waggit stuck out his nose. He sniffed tentatively. Nothing—no familiar smell tickled his supersensitive nostrils. He repeated the process on the third, fourth, and fifth floors. Now he was getting worried. Maybe he was in the wrong building. It looked like the one they always entered, but like so many things in the

world of humans, to him the buildings all seemed con-
fusingly similar. Then the doors opened on the sixth
floor. Yes, there it was, the scent of the woman, faint,
but definitely there.

He walked out of the elevator into the hallway.
There were six or seven doors on each floor, but he
had no difficulty finding the one where they lived.
With a dog's amazing sense of smell, he followed the
trail as it got stronger and stronger to one of the
brown doors, from which poured the familiar odors,
not just of her, but of the furniture, the rugs, his bed,
and all the other contents of the place that he now
called home.

It was clear from the level of the woman's scent that
she had not yet returned. Waggit tried and tried to
think of a way of entering the apartment, but nothing
came to him. If he could only get inside she wouldn't
even know that he had been to the park that night.
However, it seemed impossible. There was no window
that could be forced open, only a door in the wall with
a doormat in front of it that said A SPOILED DOG LIVES
HERE, which fortunately Waggit couldn't read. There
was nothing to do but to settle down and wait, and
receive whatever punishment she would mete out

when she returned. In all honesty this wasn't a very scary prospect, since the strictest the woman had ever been with him was to stamp her foot and yell "bad boy."

The "Spoiled Dog" doormat seemed the most logical place to lie down and wait, not to mention the most comfortable. However, lying down for dogs is a three-stage process. First the area about to be lain down on has to be prepared by scratching furiously at it. Following the preparation the animal has to turn around at least three times before the final stage, the actual lying down, can be considered. It was during the turning around part of the process that Waggit bumped his rear end against the door, and to his amazement it swung open. He looked to see if anyone was inside, but as far as he could make out, the apartment was empty. Then he suddenly realized what had happened: when she had come back to retrieve the forgotten cell phone, the woman had pulled the door shut behind her, but in her hurry had failed to check that it had fully closed. It looked shut, but obviously the lock hadn't engaged. His first reaction to this realization was relief that he could now get inside the apartment, but his second was one of irritation. Had he known that the door was open he could've saved himself the scary and dangerous trip down the fire escape.

But he could now wait for the woman's return on the comfort of his own bed and behind the security of a closed door. He made sure of the latter once he was inside by leaning heavily against it until he heard the click of the lock falling into place. He then went over to the squishy bed, repeated the lying down process, and breathed a sigh of contentment.

He fell asleep almost immediately. Saying good-bye to the team and sticking to his decision had been difficult for him, and now he was exhausted. Lowdown's voice, telling him that it would be the last time they would meet, echoed through his head. At that moment what he was giving up seemed more real to him than what he was gaining, and he was beginning to regret having gone back to the park, even though it was probably the right thing to have done. His slumber was broken by the sound of the woman's key in the lock, and he leapt to his feet, tail wagging furiously, to greet her.

As she came in the apartment Waggit knew that he had made the right decision. She was a large woman, not just physically, but in every way. She was generous, loud, warm, and affectionate. She didn't just move, but flowed like the waterfall in the park that went into the Deepwater.

"Parker my boy! What a nice welcome," she said in her voice that had been trained to be heard by large audiences and which she barely modulated for this audience of one.

She sat down on the floor, and Waggit buried himself in her, licking her face, his whole body wriggling with delight. When he first started living with her he had worried that enjoying the comfort and security she provided was a bad thing, that it was in some way shameful. He had since come to realize that most dogs needed to feel safe. That was why teams existed and why loners were so strange. He felt certain that many of his friends in the park would have done what he had done if they could have. In fact Tazar himself had said so. There was nothing to be ashamed about in feeling the way he did if that was what he really wanted. He had proved to himself and to the other team members that he could survive the hardships of life in the park, and that he was as brave as any dog in the team. Choosing a comfortable life with a woman who clearly loved him was not cowardly, and in fact the decision to stay with her took much of the same courage that he had displayed as a hunter.

The woman looked into his eyes as she stroked that special place behind the ears.

"You have become so important to me," she said. "You make my life complete. I hope that we're together for a long, long time."

Waggit looked back at her. He didn't understand her words, and even if he had, they wouldn't have meant much to him. Dogs don't think much about the future beyond the day ahead, or sometimes just the next meal. For them it is the moment that counts, and at that moment it seemed to Waggit that *his* life would be complete if the woman scratched his stomach. He rolled over onto his back and she willingly cooperated. As she watched him enjoy the sensation she could swear that he was smiling. And, you know, maybe he was.

GLOSSARY

Bad water: Gasoline

Bigwater: The reservoir

The Cold White: Snow

Curlytails: Squirrels

Deepwater: The lake

Deepwoods End: The north end of the park

Eyes and ears: Sentry duty

Feeder: Restaurant

Flutters: Birds

Goldenside: The west side of the park

The Great Unknown: The dog pound

Hoppers: Rabbits

Loners: Dogs with no team

The Long Cold: Winter

Longlegs: Horses

Luggers: Carriages pulled by horses

Nibblers: Mice

Petulants: Pet dogs

Realm: Area of the park that is the domain of a team

Rising: Day

Risingside: The East side of the park

Rollers: Cars

Rollerway: Road going through the park

Ruzelas: Anyone in authority—rangers, police, etc.

Scurries: Rats

Silver claws: Knives

Skurdie: A homeless person in the park

Skyline End: The south end of the park

Stoners: Teenage boys

Uprights: Human beings